M000285618

WOMAN SCORNED

RICK WOOD

BLOOD SPLATTER PRESS

RICK WOOD

Rick Wood is a British writer born in Cheltenham.

His love for writing came at an early age, as did his battle with mental health. After defeating his demons, he grew up and became a stand-up comedian, then a drama and English teacher, before giving it all up to become a full-time author.

He now lives in Loughborough, where he divides his time between watching horror, reading horror, and writing horror.

ALSO BY RICK WOOD

The Sensitives
The Sensitives
My Exorcism Killed Me
Close to Death
Demon's Daughter
Questions for the Devil
Repent
The Resurgence
Until the End

Blood Splatter Books
Psycho B*tches
Shutter House
This Book is Full of Bodies
Home Invasion
Haunted House
Woman Scorned

Cia Rose

When the World Has Ended
When the End Has Begun
When the Living Have Lost
When the Dead Have Decayed

The Edward King Series

I Have the Sight
Descendant of Hell
An Exorcist Possessed
Blood of Hope
The World Ends Tonight

Anthologies

Twelve Days of Christmas Horror
Twelve Days of Christmas Horror Volume 2
Roses Are Red So Is Your Blood

Standalones

When Liberty Dies
The Death Club

Sean Mallon

The Art of Murder
Redemption of the Hopeless

Chronicles of the Infected

Zombie Attack
Zombie Defence
Zombie World

Non-Fiction

How to Write an Awesome Novel
The Writer's Room

Rick also publishes thrillers under the pseudonym Ed Grace...

Jay Sullivan

Assassin Down

Kill Them Quickly

The Bars That Hold Me

A Deadly Weapon

PART I
THE END

CHAPTER ONE

SHE BRUSHES AWAY the snow and uncovers the eulogy.

She wrote it herself. His mother said it was beautiful. His sister cried. She barely blinked.

It's not that she isn't sad. She's devastated.

But she's been devastated for a long time now, and she's seen that devastation through to the end.

Is that what this is? The end?

Does everything have to end?

She snorts a laugh.

Yes, it does.

Everything has to end, and she ended it.

A few dog walkers stroll by on the nearby path. Weeds spread from the grass to the gravel and it's hard to tell where the path begins. One dog walker glances at her, but the others don't.

People often look at her, but don't want to give away that they are looking at her. So they stare in secret. They want to analyse this wretch without giving themselves away.

But the wretch doesn't care.

They can look. They can stare. They can judge.

It isn't that she feels numb; it's that she feels empty. She has unleashed so much rage and fury and sadness and grief that her emotions have run dry. She was full, and now she is empty.

She runs her hand down his name, like it's a sufficient substitute for running her hand down his face; but she doesn't feel the bump of his nose, or the moisture of his lips, or the stubble of his chin – she just feels stone. Rough, coarse, and unyielding.

So unlike him.

She knows that all widows feel like they'll never love again, but for her she knows this is true. It's not because of what she's lost by losing him – though that loss is huge – it's because of how much of herself she has lost since.

She believes that she has lost the ability to love.

The wicked don't love. The depraved don't love. Monsters don't love.

And that's what she is now. A monster.

Isn't she?

She started her story as a woman who stroked every cat she passed; who bought her mother flowers on Mother's Day; who mowed her elderly neighbour's lawn; who gave blood every few months.

But how has she ended her story?

Once, she had felt all the love in the world. She felt it both hard and soft, both gentle and harsh. Now every emotion she's ever had has drained out of her like blood down a plug hole.

But she did it out of love, didn't she?

It was all out of love for *him*. For what they did to *him*.

And for what they did to her.

Things that no one should ever have to endure.

So surely, if what she's done is because of love, she must one day be capable of love again?

Or maybe there'll never be an *again*. Maybe this truly is where her story ends.

It rains. A few drops hit her face – warning shots – then the salvo of sleet falls from the clouds.

It doesn't deter her.

If anything, she loves it.

It washes away the dirt and the filth and the hate.

No, wait.

That's not right.

It doesn't wash away the hate. Of course it doesn't. Revenge doesn't end because it's over.

Vengeance lasts a lifetime.

And so she lifts her head back. Closes her eyes. Feels the pellets of water pound her face – pummelling her skin until her cheeks are red and her hair is soaked and it's in her eyes and it's washing away the blood from her dress.

She wore a dress for him.

He always liked her in dresses.

She stands. A sudden movement that takes her by surprise; an abrupt stretch of her legs into an upright position.

She tells him she loves him.

She tells him she misses him.

And she tells him he can rest easy now.

And she leaves.

But we don't follow her. We stay with the grave.

We stay with *him*.

Because, you see, it is with *him* that our story begins.

Just as it will be with *him* that the story ends.

And now we shall begin.

PART II
THE LOVERS

MICHAEL'S STORY

CHAPTER TWO

I HAVE NEVER BEEN what one might call a 'man's man.'

Nor have I ever been a *lad*, nor could you ever accuse me of toxic masculinity. I have never thrown a punch in my life, and I have never referred to a woman as a 'bird', or a group of women as 'pussy.'

I was raised in a household where I wasn't allowed pictures of scantily clad women on my bedroom walls, as my father deemed it offensive to my mother and sister. I never had close male friends, as I've never been quite sure what to say to other men – and despite being quite good at football, I never joined a team for fear I wouldn't fit in with lad culture.

I am a man who has always been outside the circle of men. It's as if other men have this huge secret society, where they have some secret information I'm not privy to that explains why they objectify women, or make inappropriate comments to their female colleagues, or think that a woman in a night club is only there to satisfy their sexual whims.

Perhaps I've never quite understood it, or perhaps I'm just strange. Probably the latter. That's what I was always told by other boys at school. They would taunt me with accusations of homosexuality, questions about the presence of my penis, and supplying me with fake prescriptions for 'two testicles.' In all fairness, that last one is relatively amusing, when you think about it. It was probably the cleverest thing they came up with – far cleverer than "you're a bender."

My father always told me to stand up for myself, but I never did. I was too scared that they'd punch me and I'd shatter like glass. The idea of getting hurt physically was enough of a deterrent to make me just put my head down and try to ignore them.

To this day, I have never come close to being in a fight. I dread conflict. When Lisa is unhappy with me, I beg her to tell me what's wrong so I can apologise for it, no matter what it is.

So I guess that is the one thing you need to know about me before my story starts – that I am not a *lad,* and I never will be.

It has always seemed to put me at a disadvantage with women. I don't think women want a nice guy. I mean, they think they do, yet they always go out with dicks. I can't count the amount of female friends who have said to me, "I wish I could find a guy like you," whilst I sit there thinking, *you have – I am right here!*

"Mr Lister?"

A child snaps me out of my daydream. I sit up and look at her. The label pokes out of the back of her jumper, and a smear of whatever she had for lunch remains on her cheek.

"Yes, Daisy?"

"I've finished."

She presents her work for me, laying out a painting on my desk. I try to decipher what it is. The paint has run across the page into random splodges. I try turning it on its side, but it still doesn't become clear. But I can see yellow and green. Maybe it's a flower.

"That is lovely," I tell her. "Really, really lovely."

She beams.

"Now start clearing your stuff away, we're going to pack up in a minute."

She carries her artwork to her desk as paint runs off the paper and onto her trousers.

I look around at my class of year four students and survey the mess. I hate doing art with them. It wrecks my classroom. But, of course, we have to provide a 'varied syllabus' – whatever that means. Basically, I'm just allowing my classroom to be wrecked so we can keep Ofsted happy.

I sigh. Glance at the clock. There are still fifteen minutes until the end of the day, but I know it will take at least that to clean this place up – or, at least, 'clean this place up' by the standards of eight-to-nine-year-olds.

"Right, folks," I say, standing up and clasping my hands together.

None of them look up.

"We're going to start packing away now," I say, a little bit louder.

They continue painting.

"If you could please take your brushes to the sink, then put your art on the side," I repeat, loud enough that the classroom next door could probably hear me.

None of the children even lift their heads.

I bow my head. What are we even learning in this lesson? How to make the best mess? How to leave my classroom in such a state that it creates extra work for me?

"Right, I have a sweety for whoever clears up the best!"

And now they start packing away, hurrying, desperate to collect their reward.

Then I worry that I don't have any sweeties left...

I check my desk draw. There are a few jellybeans in a packet next to the lunch I didn't have time to eat. Phew.

I notice that a few students are still painting. I try to coerce them into packing away, but they don't even look up at me. I speak louder, and my voice simply gets lost in the chaos of the classroom.

I don't even feel annoyed. I'm used to it.

A crying child rushes up to me with her pig tails flapping around, pushing words out between her sniffles: "Mr" *sniff* "Lister" *sniff* "Dave" *sniff* "put" *sniff* "his" *sniff* "art" *sniff* "work" *sniff* "on" *sniff* "mine!"

"Mr Lister!" Dave – the accused – shouts, storming over. "Chloe pushed me!"

I sigh. Check the clock. Wow, it only took two minutes of packing away for the first fallout.

I remind myself that the day will be over soon, and Lisa and I will be driving away for our honeymoon, and I won't have to settle anymore childish disputes.

"Dave, take your artwork and put it somewhere else."

"But she pushed me!"

"I'm sure she's sorry, now take your artwork and–"

"I said she pushed me!"

"Okay, but you–"

"Mr Lister she's looking at me!"

"Yes, David, I heard you, but I'm sure her pushing you was a reaction to her artwork being damaged. Now, please, take your artwork and put it somewhere else."

Dave storms away. Chloe is still rubbing her eyes. The tears have ended, but she's trying to force more out. Evidently, she hasn't been given enough sympathy yet.

I take the box of tissues from my desk. It's almost empty, despite buying it only three days ago.

"Here," I say, giving her some tissues. She wipes her eyes. "Let's go see about your artwork."

She takes me to her artwork. It isn't ruined. Not that one could really tell the difference between her ruined artwork and her not-ruined artwork, but there is nothing smudged or wrecked as far as I can see. We place it on the side to dry, then she finally starts packing away her things.

I can hear another student calling from behind me. "Mr Lister, Mr Lister!" I walk away and pretend not to hear them. I care dearly about these students, but they do like to take trivial problems and make them sound like fatalities in a warzone.

Ten minutes after they are supposed to have left, I look outside my classroom window and see a crowd of impatient parents glaring in my direction. The class have finally finished clearing away their artwork and are stood in a line. I tell them to have a lovely half-term break, and off they go.

I turn back to my classroom. The tables are covered in paint, despite having laid newspaper on them. There are paint trays that haven't been cleaned, stacked on top of one another next to the sink. There are brushes on the floor beside the sink. There is paint on the chairs and on the floor. Someone has left their lunchbox on a desk. And my head is pounding.

It takes me half an hour to finish tidying up – the half an hour I was supposed to use to get a quick bit of marking done before heading home to pack.

I mean, just... why do we have to do art?

CHAPTER THREE

My COLLEAGUES TELL me they hope I have a lovely holiday, and I say the same to them. I set off home, excited to leave for my and Lisa's honeymoon.

Lisa and I were married seven weeks ago but, due to our teaching commitments, we haven't been able to go on our honeymoon until now, and I can't wait. The wedding itself was an intimate affair. Neither of us particularly like how weddings are just a way of showing a family's status – we wanted something low key, with just our closest family and friends; something that celebrated our love rather than showed off how much money we have.

I proposed at some remains in North Yorkshire called Fountains Abbey, and we decided this would be the perfect place to get married. We erected a large tent in the adjacent field for the meal, but the Easter sun was beaming down on us and, with fairy lights decorating the path, we were able to have our ceremony in the actual remains. Of course, we had to pop to the registry office in between the ceremony and the meal, as the ruins of the old monastery didn't have a marriage license – but we did this with just us and our parents. After the meal we had a ceilidh band, and we had our first dance to Ellie Goulding's cover of *Your Song*, and the whole day was just perfect.

And our honeymoon is going to be perfect too – I can feel it. A week in the middle of the countryside with just us; no annoying kids, no neighbours, nothing – just me and my soulmate.

I arrive home, walk past the white picket fence, and open the door between two hanging baskets full of red, yellow and blue flowers. I've barely taken a step before Lisa leaps on me, wraps her legs around my waist, and forces me into a kiss.

"Hi," she says, leaning her forehead against mine.

"Hi to you too."

She kisses me again. She drops down and smiles. She has the best smile. It's fiery and sexy, whilst also being sweet and cute – which pretty much sums Lisa up. She's wearing a *Jurassic Park* t-shirt and small denim shorts. She's a petite woman, is kinder than anyone I know, and more loving than I thought a person could be. And she is stunningly beautiful. And it's natural beauty – the kind of beauty you can't manufacture with clothes or makeup. But, unlike most men I know, I am just as attracted to her mind. She is intelligent, knowledgeable, and socially extroverted in a way I can't match.

I don't deserve her.

"How was your day?" she asks, her arms remaining around my neck.

"Oh, you know." I roll my eyes. "We did art again."

"Oh no. I wondered what that stain was on your shirt."

I look down at a dollop of green paint on the pocket of my shirt and roll my eyes.

"How was your day?" I ask.

"Ah, you know. Had to permanently exclude a student." Lisa works in a senior school as deputy head.

"That sucks."

"We gave him enough chances, it is what it is."

She kisses me again, then rushes into the living room, where all our bags are waiting to go in the car boot. She picks up a suitcase and a rucksack.

"You ready?"

I laugh. "Can I catch my breath first?"

She places a hand on my cheek. "I'm afraid you won't be finding many chances to catch your breath this weekend, buster – you best get used to it."

She winks at me and I get an erection. She saunters down the driveway to the car, and I can't help watching her backside as she does. She says hello to an elderly neighbour and asks whether she needs us to get her anything before we go. There is something about her that just draws other people to her – she has this relentless positive energy, and you can't help but let it affect you.

How did I get this woman?

I take two suitcases and carry them to the car, placing them in the boot next to hers.

"I'll get the last suitcase and lock up," I tell her.

"You sure?"

"Yeah, you choose what music you want."

She smiles that smile again.

I head back inside and, as I do, I notice a white van slowly passing. I look over my shoulder as the van honks its horn. A man inside, bald and wearing a vest, shouts something at Lisa.

I pause for a moment. My body paralysed with fear. Knowing I should do something to help but terrified to do so. And I hate that I'm such a coward, and that it makes me this terrified.

I tell myself that Lisa's a strong woman. That she wouldn't want me to intervene.

And I tell myself this over and over.

I check all the windows are shut, set the alarm, take the last two suitcases, lock the front door, and head to the car.

Lisa is now in the car, but the man in the white van hasn't left. His window is down and he's saying stuff to Lisa, despite her window being up. I hate his lecherous sneer, and the dribble trickling out of his mouth, and his receding hairline; but mostly I *hate* how I'm not man enough to do anything about it.

I put the suitcases in the boot, and he turns and looks at me. He's chewing gum with his mouth open, and he's missing a tooth. There is a stain on his vest, but I can't tell what it's from.

"All right, mate?" he says. He talks in a way I could never talk.

"Hi," I say, and try to avoid eye contact.

"This your bird?" he asks, nodding at Lisa.

I flinch at him calling her a *bird.*

"Yes," I mumble.

"Mate, how the fuck did you get her? She is well *fit."*

I avoid making eye contact with him as I walk to the passenger side.

I look at Lisa. She's staring straight ahead. She isn't smiling anymore.

"Are you okay?" I ask.

"I'm fine," she quickly answers.

"Do you have a shaved pussy?" the man shouts, and I just cannot understand how another man thinks it's okay to ask a woman this.

What is he trying to accomplish? He's on his own, so he's not impressing anyone. Does he think he'll get laid this way? Is this about power? Is he just thick?

I look at Lisa, who still stares straight ahead.

I want to get out and tell the man to shut up. I want to beat the hell out of him. I want to tell him that he shouldn't dare speak to my wife like that.

As it is, I just say to Lisa, "I've locked up. Shall we go?"

"Sure."

She starts the ignition and drives. The white van grows smaller in the distance.

"Are you sure you're okay?"

"I said I'm fine."

I nod and turn to the window, watching the white picket fences go by.

CHAPTER FOUR

AFTER TWENTY MINUTES OR SO, Lisa starts talking again. Five minutes later, we are laughing and joking like nothing happened, and I pretend not to feel ashamed.

We listen to a playlist Lisa made on her phone – it's called *Happy Songs*. We make up our own words to *Walking on Sunshine* and pretend to know the words to *Pack Up Your Troubles in Your Old Kit-Bag*, and we are, once again, happy. It makes me think back to our first date – we both admitted how we keep forgetting song lyrics and we made a deal that, from then on, should we forget them, we would not stop singing along, and would make them up instead. I sang alone to Celine Dion, changing the words to "my farts will linger on", and she laughed so hard she snorted and her drink came out her nose.

We met on Bumble. It's like Tinder, except the woman has to message first. Lisa was quite delicate at the time, having been in a destructive relationship beforehand. The few times her ex has come up in conversation, she's talked about how he was the complete opposite of me. A laddish, domineering alpha male. Someone who's attracted to her youthful exuberance because it's something he could destroy. Someone who was so arrogant that he believed that he was better than everyone and everything.

I looked him up once, and found that he's in prison now, though Lisa would never tell me that; she's always trying to protect me. Like when she pretends that she never looks at another man, or that she never gets hit on in a bar. As if I'm too fragile to take it. But it's okay – it's how she keeps me safe.

I met her just as I finished my teacher training, and I was struggling to find a job. Her father was the headmaster at the local primary school, and he helped me get a maternity cover job, then made it permanent. I've applied for a senior role a few times, but he always gives the job to someone else – most recently, a small but overweight woman who is brilliant at dealing with behavioural issues. Perhaps he thinks I'm too sensitive. I'm fairly sure he only gave me the job because Lisa begged him to. Yet another thing she's done for me. I only wish there was something I could do for her that would have the same kind of impact she's had on me.

But she doesn't need me to do anything for her. She doesn't need anyone to. She's a strong person who achieves everything she wants without help from anyone else. Sometimes I wonder why she married someone so useless. But she seems happy.

"What are you lost in thought about?" she asks.

"Oh, nothing. Just… thinking."

"About what?"

I look at her. The sunlight illuminates her freckles. She's never looked so perfect.

What does she see in me? She could have anyone, so why choose an insecure fool?

Stop it. Those thoughts aren't helpful. She chose to marry me. She wants *me*.

Really, she does.

"Just thinking about our honeymoon. Wondering if this place is as good as you say."

"Honestly, I went to Frome as a child, and it was the best holiday I ever had."

I try not to think about whether that includes the three holidays she's been on with me.

"But I looked it up on Google Maps," I tell her. "It looks like it's in the middle of nowhere."

"It is in the middle of nowhere! There's field after field, pubs where everyone knows each other, no shops for ages. We can really be alone."

"Sounds like the opening of a horror movie. Where will we get milk if there's no shops?"

"Oh, there's a post office. I think it's their only communication with the outside world."

I chuckle. "Sounds great."

We leave the motorway after half an hour, drive across an A road for a bit, then spend the next twenty minutes driving along country lanes. It really is in the middle of nowhere.

"Oh, dammit," Lisa says.

"What?"

"The oil light's come on. I forgot to do it earlier."

"Will we last until we get to the cottage?"

"Yeah, but we might want to use the car again. Let's just find a garage."

I put *mechanic* into Google Maps, and it creates a route to the nearest one. Surprisingly, it isn't that far away, considering we've not seen a single other car since we left the A36.

Five minutes later, we pull up to the garage. It doesn't look like much. The workshop is an open space with a few cars inside, next to a small shop with a till on a desk. Above the shop are faded letters where the name of the garage used to be. I think I can make out an R and a P. A man, possibly early forties, stands outside, smoking. He wears a jumpsuit, and has a tattoo of a red cross on his neck that I'm pretty sure is the symbol for the English Defence League.

Lisa brings the car to a stop. We get out.

And this is where it all starts to go wrong.

CHAPTER FIVE

It's a quick oil and filter change. That's all it is.

The man in the jumpsuit walks toward us. A head like a boulder. Stomping like a bull. Snorting as his large frame wobbles forward. He takes our keys, drives the car into the shop, and says something to a woman. She looks at us and sniggers. He gives her a kiss. She lifts the bonnet and gets to work. She's also wearing a jumpsuit and has tribal tattoos up her neck, and a cross tattooed beside her eye. Her hair is black, and in a ponytail.

The man returns to the wall and finishes his cigarette, dropping ash on his thick, black boots. We lean awkwardly against a fence, not sure how long we're supposed to wait, or where we are supposed to stand.

He doesn't even glance in our direction.

A few minutes later, a small, filthy car swings around the corner and skids to a halt. A man steps out. Shaved head, a cobweb tattooed under his eye, and an arrogant swagger to his walk. He has the kind of vacant smile on this face that you normally see on stupid people who don't realise how stupid they are.

"Yo, Pitbull, you cunt!" he says to the man learning against the wall. "How's it going?"

Pitbull grins, engages his friend in a raised handshake, and they nudge their shoulders together.

"Good, Jonno, you?"

I raise my eyebrows at this man being called *Pitbull,* and for Jonno's term of endearment for him being *cunt.* I consider how unlikely I am to ever be nicknamed *Pitbull,* or be friends with someone nicknamed *Pitbull.* Or even *Jonno.*

Lisa called me *puppy* once, and that's probably the closest I'll get.

"All right, Kacey?" Jonno shouts into the shop. Kacey raises a hand to say hello as she works on our car.

Jonno puts his hands down the crotch of his grey tracksuit bottoms, and this is where he leaves them. As if that's normal.

He turns and sees us. Looks Lisa up and down. Smirks. Widely. Like he knows something we don't.

He turns back to Pitbull and they share a smirk. Like they both know something, and I don't quite get it.

"I'm done," Kacey shouts after a few minutes.

The one called Pitbull nods his head toward us and walks through a door. I take my wallet out and follow him into a small shop, no bigger than our kitchen.

"That's one hundred and eight," he says.

"How much?"

"Hundred and eight."

"For an oil and filter change?"

Pitbull's head tilts to the side. He narrows his eyes.

"Yeah. That's what I said, ennit?"

He stares at me, and I see his stare for what it is: a threat. The look of a predator warning its prey. He's waiting for me to challenge him, for me to ask why it is so much, for me to refuse to pay it.

I present my credit card.

He puts it in the reader, then holds the reader high to get signal. I wait. After what seems like an excessive wait, he presents it to me and grunts, "Pin."

I cover the numbers with one hand and enter my pin. His grin widens.

He holds the machine high again, and waits. Eventually, a receipt comes out, which he pulls off and hands to me, along with my card.

"Have a lovely day," he says, again with that knowing grin, like his wish for us to have a nice day is something sinister.

"Cheers," I say, take my card and receipt, and leave.

When I step outside, I see Jonno. Stood next to Lisa.

No, not *next to*, actually – he is stood over her. She is facing away, and his body is against her arm, and he's chewing open-mouthed, his hands still resting on his crotch, saying something into her ear.

Lisa rubs her arms, looking uncomfortable.

"Are you okay?" I ask her as I approach.

Jonno turns away from her and toward me. Gives me the same grin Pitbull gave me.

"Mate, you got a good-looking bird here."

"Thanks," I mutter, then wonder why I said it. I'm not grateful. I'm not happy with him harassing my wife. I don't want the compliment. So why the hell did I thank him?

Kacey drives our car out of the shop and parks it next to us.

Lisa walks away from Jonno, past me, and into the car.

Kacey gives me the keys and I turn to go. Then I feel it. Jonno's hand on my shoulder.

I turn to look at him, and my entire body seizes, gripped with fear; absolute terror for what this man is going to do.

"You have a good night," he says. "Enjoy that pussy."

He finally lets go of my shoulder. Gives me a wink. Waits to see how I'm going to react.

I walk away from him and get in the car, and I wonder why it is that men like him seem to bother us. Do I appear so timid and unmanly that other men don't see me as a threat, even when I am standing with my wife? Or is it simply because I am *a nice guy* – a term that rarely sparks arousal in the opposite sex.

I hand Lisa the keys and she drives away. I watch them disappear in the mirror, and I feel like I can still hear the open-mouthed slops of Jonno chewing his gum.

Lisa sets off so quickly she doesn't have a chance to put the cottage back into Google Maps, so I do it for her, and the directions resume.

After a minute or so, I put my hand on her leg, and I say, "I'm sorry."

She glances at me, confused.

"For what?"

It's a good question. What am I sorry for?

"For... him. That guy. The other guy. All guys, I guess."

It makes her laugh. So I laugh too.

"I know I should stand up for–"

"I can stand up for myself."

"I know you can. It's just not okay."

"That's why I married a guy who isn't like that. Didn't I?"

She shoots me a smile. I'm grateful for it, but I know it's not genuine. It's just for my sake. And I hate myself for it.

She has just been harassed, and now she's saying things to make *me* feel better. Shouldn't I be the one saying things to cheer her up?

"Let's just enjoy our honeymoon," Lisa says. "Forget about them. Where we're going, we'll barely come across anyone else, anyway."

"I know. I just..."

"Forget about it. Honestly, Michael, please, just… let's forget about it."

"Okay."

She puts the music back on. The last few tunes of the *Happy Songs* playlist blare out of the speakers.

This time, we don't sing along.

CHAPTER SIX

WHEN WE REACH THE COTTAGE, it's like nothing else matters. It's perfect. Quaint but large. Classic yet modern. Picturesque – like it belongs on a postcard –surrounded by field after field, with not a soul around.

We both get out of the car, jaws dropped, staring. Stepping stones lead us across the grass, past an outdoor seating area and blooming flower beds, and toward a porch baring a sign that reads *It's not the size of the house, but the happiness of the home.*

Inside is just as amazing – a modern interior that contrasts perfectly with the older architecture of the exterior. The evening sunshine is warm in a conservatory that contains wicker chairs ready for our coffee in the morning. The dining table is rustic, and the glass cabinets spotless. A large sofa with huge, puffy cushions waits for us inside the living area, opposite a television and a bookcase that offers a large selection of DVDs.

Once I finish looking around the place, I find Lisa in the bedroom, looking out the window. I pass the king-size bed and the large wardrobe, place my arms around her waist, and gaze over her shoulder at the view. I can see why she's staring out of this window. It's magnificent. Hills in the background, bright-green fields nearby, and a lake with a steady stream in the distance.

"It's amazing," she says.

"It is. It's what you deserve."

She turns to me and places her arms around my neck. "It's what *we* deserve."

I look into her eyes – those big, blue eyes – and despite her youthful appearance, I still see wisdom in them. I see strength. I see courage. I see a woman who wouldn't want me to stick up to that arsehole at the mechanics, or that dickhead in the white van – I see a woman who does not need a protector. She simply needs a companion.

"I love you," I tell her.

"I love you, too."

I pray that our marriage will last. I know this is how all relationships start out – happy and hopeful. But that isn't how they all end. You just need to look at my parents and her parents to see the mess that can be left once a relationship becomes toxic. But I vow, silently to myself, that I will never let us fall apart like that.

My father told me on our wedding day that all marriages will have dark times, and we won't be the exception. But I know that I will keep trying – because there is nothing I want more.

I'm about to say that we still need to get the luggage out of the car when she starts kissing me. Gently, at first, then it becomes passionate. To hell with the luggage, that can wait. I move her to the bed, and her lips remain attached to mine as she unbuttons my shirt.

We have been together for years, and we must have had sex many, many times by now – but even so, it still feels special. It's still exciting. I'm still eager to remove her clothes and see what's underneath, as if I'm seeing it again for the first time.

We undress each other and she lies down and I stand up, and she says, "Are you not joining me?"

"Yeah," I say. "I am, I just… I want to capture the moment."

She laughs. I know I'm a dork. Only weirdos pause foreplay and use the words *capture the moment.* But I don't care. She's naked. Laying over the bed sheets, with her small, perky breasts lying to the side. Her belly rises and sinks. Her hair spreads over the pillow. Her curved thighs are apart, waiting for me.

I climb over her and we kiss again. Then I move my lips to her neck. To her breasts. I run my tongue down her belly and to the inside of her thigh. She's begging me and I oblige, rubbing my tongue over her clitoris. Five minutes later, my fingers are inside of her and my tongue is quickly moving in the shape of the alphabet and she is coming.

She turns me over and places me in her mouth and it only takes minutes until I'm ready. She moves on top, places me inside of her, and smiles as she feels it. She moves back and forth, holding her head over mine, and her hair drops over me, trapping us in a beautiful prison.

Then she leans up, spreads her chest, and I marvel at the beauty of her nudity again. She moves her hips back and forth, and she knows just how to move to make both of us shake.

She grunts harder, and she breathes quicker, and I know she's close, so I allow myself to be close, and together we scream.

When it's over, she doesn't move away. She stays there, keeping me inside of her, looking me in the eyes. We kiss, and she doesn't let me out until I'm completely limp, at which point she rolls to the side and lays there in sweaty delight. I put my arm around her and pull her close, and in this moment I do not care about other guys looking at her, or hitting on her, or seeing me as such a dweeb that they can just brush me aside – right now, there is just me and her, in our own world full of poetry and love.

"That was fantastic," she says.

"Oh, I know. I was there."

We laugh. She nestles into the underside of my arm, placing her arm across my chest.

And we lay there.

After a while, we have a shower, and put on the large, fluffy dressing gowns left in the wardrobe. We have pasta for tea, and we don't wear anything but those dressing gowns for the rest of the night.

When we go to sleep, we lie on our sides with my arms around her, and that is how we fall asleep. Like two perfect circles wrapped around each other.

CHAPTER SEVEN

THE CHAIR IS leather with wooden legs. It sits in the corner of Pitbull and Kacey's bedroom, and it's where he likes to sit while his wife fucks other men.

This boy is tall. A bit gangly. Maybe early twenties. His penis isn't as big as Pitbull's, but not many men's are. Kacey is moaning on every thrust, but Pitbull is sure this is a performance for his benefit. In truth, the lad hasn't been that great. But it doesn't matter. It is being watched that arouses Kacey, and it is the jealousy that turns Pitbull on. Watching his naked wife, late thirties but still desired by a younger man, as her sex face – a contortion of what looks like shock and discomfort – peers up at the stranger Pitbull invited home.

The bloke – Pitbull forgets his name – begins to move faster, and he starts making noise.

"Do not cum," Kacey tells him.

"What?" he mutters.

"He doesn't like other men coming inside of me."

The man glances over his shoulder at Pitbull.

Pitbull, a large, beefy man with an intimidating presence,

says nothing. The scrawny boy doesn't question Kacey's instructions, and he slows down a bit.

"Fuck me from behind," Kacey says, pushes him out of her and turns over. He quickly obliges, and Pitbull watches as the boy's testicles bounce back and forth, colliding with her thighs. He stands so he's able to examine the man's penis moving in and out of her more closely. After a few minutes, he sighs and strips off. He's had enough.

Kacey sees Pitbull approaching and pushes the bloke off. Her husband enters her from behind and she screams like she doesn't scream for anyone else. A little in pleasure, and a little in pain – he does have a huge cock, after all. Pitbull doesn't thrust or penetrate his woman; he *pounds* her. Hard. Growling his manly growls as he does.

The young man stands awkwardly, watching. Not quite sure what to do, he turns around and picks up his clothes.

Pitbull looks over his shoulder at the boy and grunts, "My arsehole."

"What?" the boy asks.

"You fucking heard me!"

The boy looks back and forth, not sure what this means.

"*Now!*" Pitbull shouts.

The boy doesn't wait any longer. He rubs his penis, stiffening his erection, and takes some lubricant from the bedside table. He sprays it over his small cock and all over Pitbull's anus, then tries to insert his penis inside of it. With Pitbull's large thrusts, it's not easy, but the boy is too scared to admit defeat, so he perseveres – and, eventually, Pitbull feels the man fill him just as he fills his wife. He grows even harder, and Kacey's screams grow louder, enjoyment of both the bliss and the pain.

Pitbull concentrates on the feel of this boy scraping his insides. It feels like an enjoyable shit, and it tingles as the boy reaches his prostate, and he loves it, and it turns him on even more to look down and see himself gaining sensations from both ends.

"Cum in me," he says, looking over his shoulder at the boy.

The boy looks reluctant, but doesn't dare disobey. He goes faster and Pitbull goes faster and, just as he feels the boy's erection expand and convulse, his expands also, and he roars and he growls and snorts and they ejaculate together, just as Kacey's screams are also brought to a crescendo.

When they are done, Pitbull pushes the boy away, and he falls to the floor. He remains inside of Kacey for a moment, then pulls out and shoves her onto her back.

He takes a huge clump of tissue and begins wiping the end of his cock.

The boy stands and looks timidly at the married couple.

"What?" Pitbull says.

"I, er…"

"What you looking at?"

"Well, erm, I don't–"

"Fuck off."

"What?"

"You didn't hear me? I said fuck off – we're done with you."

The boy looks at Kacey, who grins at him. She knows this is how his night ends. He quickly gathers his clothes.

"*Now!*"

Pitbull grows impatient. He isn't interested in having breakfast with the boy. His part is over and there's no reason for him to still be here.

The boy rushes out of the room and gets dressed as he runs down the stairs. Moments later, they hear the front door hastily open and shut.

Pitbull turns to Kacey and smiles as he finishes wiping himself off.

Some of his cum drools out of her cunt and onto the mattress.

He climbs onto the bed and lies next to her, says, "That boy was shit," and they both laugh.

"Maybe you should have fucked him," she whispers.

"A kid like that? A cock like mine would rip his arsehole open."

They laugh again. Then they fall silent. It isn't long before Pitbull is snoring.

Kacey gets up, pulls the duvet over him, and has a shower before climbing into bed herself.

CHAPTER EIGHT

I WAKE IN THE MORNING, open the curtains, and marvel at the sunny view. I still can't believe we get to stay here for a whole week. Lisa's friends made fun of us for staying in the UK for our honeymoon, but this is the kind of view you won't get in many other places. It would be a great place to go for a run, too. In fact, I decide to do just that.

I put on my t-shirt and shorts, then pop to the toilet. When I come out of the bathroom, I find Lisa wearing her t-shirt and shorts too.

"Are you going for a run?" I ask, chuckling.

"Yeah – this will be a great place to go for a run, don't you think?"

I laugh. She asks why, and I tell her, and she laughs too, and we agree to go for a run together.

I used to hate those couples who would get up in the morning and go for a run. I'd drive past them on the way to work and wonder what was wrong with them. Now look at me.

Doesn't love make you silly?

We set off along the country road that led to our house,

then spot a Public Footpath sign next to a field. We climb over the stile and run along the field's edge until we meet the lake. The sun glistens in the clear water, and its sound is hypnotic – like those ambient meditation sounds Lisa sometimes listens to before bed.

I could get used to this.

We carry on past a stream, go up the hill, and I persevere through a bit of aching. I haven't gone for as many runs as Lisa recently, and she doesn't seem that bothered about the slope.

Once we reach the top of the hill, we pause, and I lean over, waiting for my panting to subside. I wipe sweat from my brow, then see Lisa standing at the hill's edge.

I join her, and together we marvel at the view.

"Wow," I say.

"I know."

Various shades of green spread further into the distance, field after field. Beyond those are a few houses, small, distant, and indistinct.

"Is that Frome?" she asks.

"I guess so. I think this is Cley Hill – I read about these views."

"It's incredible."

"Yeah."

She looks at me. She kisses me.

"What was that for?"

She smiles cheekily. "Let's get back home and you might find out."

"Oh yeah?"

"You think you've got a sweat on now, you haven't seen anything, buster…"

She winks at me. Suddenly, I have a lot more energy. She carries on running, and I follow, and we go back down the slope of the hill.

When we return to the bottom, we slow our run down to a

jog, then into a brisk walk, allowing our bodies to adjust as we approach the country road that will take us back to the cottage.

That is when we realise that we aren't alone.

"Who's that?" Lisa asks.

"I dunno," I say, though I recognise him.

He's sat on the stile that we need to climb over. He has something in his hands. He's on his own, but that doesn't stop him from sniggering as if someone's beside him.

"It's that guy from the garage," Lisa says. She's right. The man who was leant over Lisa when I walked out. The slimy, disgusting guy. I think his name was Jonno.

"For God's sake," Lisa groans. "Are these guys just following me around?"

It certainly feels like it.

"Ah, well, we have to go past him," Lisa says. "May as well just do it."

She takes a deep breath and walks toward him.

My entire body seizes with fear. Which is ridiculous. Lisa is the one he was harassing, yet she's the one confidently striding toward him, and I'm the one shaking with terror.

What is it I'm so scared of? That he's going to punch me? Humiliate me? Push me to the ground?

…Yes, actually.

That is *exactly* what I'm worried about.

It's what I worry about every time I walk past a 'lad', and each time I feel more and more pathetic.

I take a deep breath, keep my eyes on him, and follow Lisa.

As we get closer, I can see what he has in its hands. It's a lighter. And a cat. Jesus, he's holding the cat still in one hand, and holding the lighter to its belly with the other. And he's laughing at it.

The bloody guy is laughing at it.

"Oh, my God," Lisa gasps.

Now I feel even more scared. I know Lisa won't let this go. She loves animals. She used to volunteer for the RSPCA before she began teacher training. I'd even promised her we can get a dog during the summer. She will be enraged as to what this guy is doing, and she will not let him carry on doing it.

And I am terrified as to what he'll do when she tries to stop him.

She marches toward him before I can object – not that I would even try – and I walk briskly to keep up with her.

"Excuse me!" she demands.

Jonno ignores her. He holds the cat high by the skin of its neck and takes the flame of his lighter to its paw. The cat squeals and struggles, but can't get away.

"Excuse me!"

He ignores her again.

"I know you can hear me!"

Jonno turns toward her. Still holding the cat. Still holding the lighter. He says nothing. Just gives her a lecherous grin.

"Whatever are you doing?"

He snorts a laugh. "You sound well posh."

"Excuse me?"

"I said, you sound well posh. Where'd you come from – Windsor or summit?"

"I don't care for what you have to say to me – put that cat down now!"

"Why?"

"Because you're hurting it."

"It's my cat."

"Well then you shouldn't be allowed it."

He puts on a posh voice. "Oh, shouldn't I?"

She turns to look at me, as if I'm going to back her up. By the time she turns back to Jonno, he's stood up, and he's holding the cat loosely at his side.

"Maybe I should put a lighter under you instead," he says.

"Just leave the cat alone. Now. I mean it!"

"You mean it?"

"Yes, I do!"

"What you going to do?"

She crosses her arms. I wish I had her courage. Or is it stupidity? I can't tell.

He finally lets go of the cat. It runs away. He flicks the lighter and lifts the flame, raising it to his eye level so he can line it up with Lisa's face.

Lisa huffs and carries on walking, but he blocks the stile.

"Now what?" he asks.

"Now we need to use that stile, if you don't mind."

He looks back at the stile. Then back at us. "Oh, do you?"

"Yes, so if you would kindly get out of the way."

He steps toward her.

I should really say something. I should help her. I know I should.

"And if I don't?" he asks.

She looks over her shoulder at me, huffs, and turns back to him.

"We would just like to go home, please."

"Home? You're a long way from home…"

Just say something, Michael. Stop being such a coward. Speak up.

"I think–" I say, and I stop immediately, hearing the wobble to my voice, then urge myself to keep going. "I think you should let us past."

He laughs at me. "Are you going to make me?"

"No. I just… We would like to use the stile."

He stands back. Opens his arm to present the stile.

Finally.

Lisa walks forward. I follow. And, as I do, he grabs my collar, and I am petrified.

"Please, just–"

I see his arm swing toward me, and the next thing I know he's landed his thick fist against my face, and I'm falling to the ground, clutching my eye. I feel Lisa's hands on my back, and I hear her asking if I'm okay, and I've never been punched before and my cheek is throbbing and I feel disorientated.

"Are you happy now?" Lisa shouts at him. "Just go away!"

Jonno laughs. Lingers. Then leaves, shaking his head at our stupidity.

She helps me to my feet, then winces as she sees my face.

"Oh, wow," she says. "I think you're going to get a black eye."

"Great. That'll look wonderful in our honeymoon pictures."

She places a hand on my cheek. "You did great. Come on, let's get some ice on it."

She leads me to the stile and, even though he only punched my cheek, it feels like my whole body now aches.

I climb over the stile and she keeps her hand on my back as we walk home.

CHAPTER NINE

IT'S past midday on Saturday by the time Pitbull wakes up. He climbs out of bed, opens the curtains, and gazes out of the window as his flaccid dick waves to and fro. The sun shines on the weeds that tangle around a set of wooden panels he left on the grass when he fixed the fencing a few months ago. It looks like it's going to be a nice day.

He glances over his shoulder. Kacey lays in bed, the cover around her ankles, her breasts laying to the side, her body glistening with sweat, her cunt still wet. He considers fucking her again, but he's thirsty, so he walks downstairs, to the fridge, opens the whole milk and drinks it from the carton. A bit dribbles down his chin and onto his chest. He doesn't give a shit.

A pounding on the door interrupts his drinking. He puts the milk back in the fridge and opens it.

"All right," Jonno says, walking in with a four-pack of beer. He hands one to Pitbull, takes one for himself, and puts the other two in the fridge.

He wipes morning perspiration from his forehead onto his

vest as he takes a seat in the kitchen and puts his feet up on the dining table.

"All right," Pitbull replies, opening his lager and taking a few gulps as he watches a neighbour walk past with her pram. There's something about single mothers that just really does it for him.

"You will not guess who I ran into this morning!" Jonno proclaims

Pitbull sits down and puts his feet on the dining table next to Jonno's. He opens his bare legs so his sweaty cock can breathe.

"Who?" he grunts, and takes another large swig. It's good beer.

"You remember that bloke and that bird at the shop yesterday?"

Pitbull shrugs.

"You know, that prissy little thing. Fit but frigid. Bit posh."

"The couple?"

"Yeah, the couple."

"I remember."

"I ran into them today. I was playing with Tibbles and that, and she got all in my face about it."

Pitbull takes another swig and waits for Jonno to reach the point of his story.

"I only went and gave the bloke a black eye, didn't I?" he says, laughing.

Pitbull frowns. "Why?"

"They tried to act all high and mighty on me, like. Telling me what I can do. Acting like they are smart and all that. The fucking up-themselves-pricks."

Kacey walks in, as naked as her husband, her feet pattering across the kitchen tiles. Her hair is messy and her nipples are hard. She takes a beer from the fridge.

"All right, Jonno," she says, taking a gulp of her lager.

"All right, Kacey, what's happening?"

"Not much. Did I hear you saying you gave that bloke a black eye?"

Jonno cackles. "Yeah, I did."

She laughs.

"And that bird, man," Jonno continues. "I tell you what, as up herself as she is, you don't get pussy like that round here. I mean, most women round here are either retired bitches in their seventies, or women with no teeth who fuck their daddies."

Pitbull grimaces. "Kacey ain't like that."

"Ah, well, our Kacey here's just the exception, ain't she?"

Kacey smiles, takes another swig of her lager, announces she's going to have a bath, and leaves the room.

"I tell you what though," Jonno says, taking his feet off the table and leaning toward Pitbull. "I would give my left nut to have a go on that bitch."

"She was good-looking."

"Good-looking? Good-looking don't do it justice, mate."

"Yeah, she was real nice."

"Mate, she was fit as fuck. She's just Kacey's type, too."

Pitbull thinks about this.

Kacey likes a small, petite women. The delicate ones. The ones that might break under a little pressure. The ones who would be damaged by the experience. She likes to turn them into *real women,* as she puts it – and Pitbull likes to watch.

And nothing would give him more pleasure than watching Kacey break this woman.

He wonders…

"I know where they're staying, too," Jonno announces. "Up in that cottage, you know; the one at the bottom of Cley Hill."

"Is that a fact?"

"Tempted to pay them a visit, you know what I mean?"

Pitbull does know what Jonno means.

Then Pitbull remembers his age. He's twenty years older than Jonno, and only keeps the guy around because he reminds Pitbull of his younger days – the days when he would join other West Ham fans in kicking a Millwall fan's teeth in – when he would come onto a woman in the night club and not give her a choice – when having a tattoo was still cool and not a mid-life crisis.

But those days are gone. Now it's afternoons in the beer garden and evenings listening to autobiographies of ex-gangsters.

"Let's just get some food," Pitbull says. "Let's get some beers, maybe a chippy. Forget about that couple. They ain't worth it."

"Fine – but, like I said, she's real lively. She would be a good catch."

"Yeah, maybe – but she ain't special."

She isn't special.

Kacey is special.

All other women are just a means to an end.

So Pitbull tries to think of things other than this woman and her husband, and the things they could do to them, and the pleasure he would derive from it – but it will be all he can think about all day.

CHAPTER TEN

I SPEND most of the morning sitting on the porch with an ice pack on my face.

I am determined not to let this ruin our honeymoon, but I am shaken up. My legs are wobbling and my arms are trembling and I feel too scared to even leave the cottage.

Then again, are we even safe in the cottage? It wouldn't be difficult for that Jonno guy to figure out where we're staying. There's only one cottage near the bottom of that hill, and if he knows the area, surely he will know where we are.

What if he comes back? And with more people? And with weapons?

And what if they don't – but I see him next time we go for a walk? What then?

I want to go home. I want to leave this cottage, leave Frome, and go back to the house we bought together, the one where I feel safe. But I don't say this. I don't want Lisa to realise how scared I am, nor do I want to ruin the honeymoon.

But I've never been punched before, and I don't know what to do.

"Here," Lisa says, placing a cup of tea beside me, along with a sandwich. It's brie, bacon and cranberry. She knows it's my favourite. I don't deserve this woman.

"Thank you," I say, and she sits next to me and starts eating her own sandwich. I assume it's lunchtime.

"How are you feeling?" she asks.

I shrug. "In pain."

"Would you feel up to going somewhere this afternoon?"

I really don't. I'm too scared to go anywhere or do anything. But I don't want to be a burden. I don't want to force her to stay inside for the entirety of our honeymoon.

And I don't want to be such a coward.

"Maybe we should go to the police," she says.

"No. It's fine."

That would just make it worse. There's no CCTV – Jonno would just deny it, and then he'd know we've been to the police and would want to come after me.

"We could just go for a walk, then drive out and get some fish and chips and eat them in the cottage," she suggests. "Maybe snuggle up with a movie instead of going out for dinner tonight, how does that sound?"

The staying in part sounds good. Not sure about the rest. But I don't want to ruin her holiday. She's been great this morning; sitting with me, holding my hand, reassuring me, talking to me… But I know there's a point where she'll have had enough. Where she will get restless and wish to go out.

And I think we're just about to reach that point.

"Sounds good," I say. Resigned to leaving the cottage. At least in here we can lock the doors, but I can't stay behind locked doors forever.

I finish my sandwich. Go to the bathroom and have a moment. Look at myself in the mirror. Regret doing so as I notice the black around my eye. I splash water on my face and remind myself again not to let it ruin our honeymoon.

But it already has.

"Get a grip," I tell myself, but it lacks conviction. My eye looks awful, and when I leave the bathroom and force a smile at Lisa, I remember that when she smiles back, she'll be looking at my eye.

We go for a walk and she holds my hand. She always wants to hold my hand. Even when we just nip out of the car to go to the cash machine, she still holds my hand. Like she wants to be seen with me. Like she wants to claim me. But why? What is it she's claiming?

She should be embarrassed to be holding hands with me.

I will the bad thoughts away and we go for a walk, following the stream. The sun remains high in the sky and her hand remains in mine. We stop at a pub – the kind of pub where everyone looks at us and wonders who these non-locals are – and have a drink. People stop staring after ten minutes or so, and I actually manage to relax. We laugh. We make fun of people we know from home. We make plans for tomorrow.

And we are *us* again.

Maybe I was overreacting. Maybe it's not so bad. It's just a black eye, right?

We return to the cottage as early evening arrives. It feels cooler, but still warm enough to sit on the porch. We share a bottle of red wine and cuddle, enjoying each other's company.

When her stomach starts to make noises, I volunteer to get the fish and chips.

"Are you sure?" she asks. "I can go if you want."

"No, it's fine. I'll go."

I need to do this. I need to go out on my own and prove to myself that I'm not going to get hurt each time I leave the safety of the cottage.

As stupid as it is, I need to be brave and go out to get some fish and chips.

I find the closest chippy on Google Maps. It's about fifteen minutes away, and I set off in the car, passing field after field.

Trees cast the country road in shadow, with leaves of lots of different colours. It's the kind of beautiful that does not exist in the city.

This isn't so bad.

It's a lovely place. I'm with the woman I love. It's our honeymoon. Sure, I have a mark on my face, but it will fade.

I actually allow myself to smile.

Then I arrive at the chippy. Park the car. Stare at the empty shop and the people waiting to serve me.

And I close my eyes. Take a deep breath. It is highly unlikely Jonno will be here. In fact, the odds are very much in favour that he won't be. There are so many places he could be that the odds are almost astronomical in my favour.

So I get out the car. My leg shakes as my feet touch the ground. By the time I get into the shop, they have stopped shaking, and I feel fine.

I order two fish and chips with a side of curry sauce and lean against the counter as they prepare my order.

I begin to relax.

And, just as I do, I see a jeep pull up outside. I recognise the people inside, and my body seizes with fear and my eyes widen at the sight of Pitbull, Kacey and Jonno.

The odds were astronomical.

They were.

Yet here they are, and I have never been more terrified.

CHAPTER ELEVEN

THE WOMAN GETS OUT. Kacey, I think. The others don't see me. I think. Or maybe they do, I don't know. But she gets out and walks in and I do my best to look the other way.

"Hey," she says to the person serving, who seems to recognise her.

"Kacey, how's it going?"

"Good, mate. Yourself?"

"Great. How's Pitbull?"

"Good."

"Sweet. What can I get you?"

"Three chips, three battered sausages, and three mushy peas."

"Coming right up."

They prepare her order. She looks around. Chewing gum with her mouth open. Why do they always chew gum? If she was my student I'd tell her to spit it out. Or would I?

Her eyes linger on me. I try to look away, but she notices the black eye and her mouth falls open.

"Aw, mate, look at that shiner!" she says.

I force a fake smile.

"How'd you do that?" Her eyes flicker with recognition. "Aw, wait, I know you – you came into the shop, didn't you?"

"Yes," I mumble.

"Yeah – you're the one with the real fit wife, ain't you?"

I don't quite know what to say to that, so I force another smile and look away.

"Jonno gave you that shiner, didn't he?" she asks, smiling and shaking her head, as if it's nothing, as if it's just *typical Jonno, he's such a silly boy, isn't he...*

I nod and keep looking away.

"Man, that Jonno, I tell you... He has problems."

"I bet."

"Man, it's just – it's a beauty. I've got to have a closer look."

She steps into my personal space and places her hands on the side of my head and turns my face toward her. She stretches my cheek and my eye. She moves her face to within inches of mine and examines the different shades of black.

"Fuuuuck... That is a real corker... I bet Jonno was well proud of that one..."

I try to look away again, but it's hard when someone is grabbing your face.

"Why didn't you slog him back?" she asks. "He's a little wuss, really. Next time, throw a fist back at him, and I bet he'll just squeal away."

"I'll keep that in mind."

The doors to the jeep open. The older, bigger bloke comes out. The one called Pitbull, though I very much doubt that's what his parents named him. The chime over the door announces his entry, and he charges up to us.

"You coming onto my wife?" he asks me, his voice low-pitched and drawn out.

"No, no, I promise, I was not!"

"Then why's she touching your face?"

"I didn't ask her to, I swear, I just want my fish and chips!"

"Pitbull, look at this," Kacey says, turning my head toward Pitbull.

"Fuck me," Pitbull exclaims, and he comes close to examine the various shades of pain as well. "That is a beauty. Jonno did that, didn't he?"

Pitbull looks over his shoulder at Jonno, who remains in the jeep, and I pray he does not come in, and I pray they just hurry up with my order.

"I was just saying how his wife is fit," Kacey says.

"Oh yeah? She is proper fit."

The server places a bag on the counter and smiles at me. I step out of Kacey's reach, take my order, and head for the door.

Pitbull steps in my way, and my body tenses.

"You like that shiner?" He asks me.

I say nothing.

"I know where you're staying," he tells me. "It's where all the snobs go. So be careful."

I don't know what I need to be careful for, but I am so grateful when Kacey says, "Ah, he's fine, let him go," and her husband finally steps aside.

I run from the shop to my car, quickly past the jeep, and lock the doors as soon as I'm in. I turn the ignition and drive away before stopping further down the road to find my route back to the cottage with Google Maps.

I am wheezing.

My breath… I'm hyperventilating.

My palms are so sweaty that my hands slip off the steering wheel.

I try to calm down, grateful for being able to leave unharmed, and I hate myself for being such a coward, but at the same time I am just so, so thankful for being able to get away.

Eventually, my breathing gets a little calmer, though my chest still hurts. I set off, afraid that they will drive past and see me.

I do not stop shaking for the entire journey.

CHAPTER TWELVE

PITBULL AND KACEY sit in the front of the jeep with open lagers and open chips on their laps. Jonno sits in the back.

No one says a word.

They just sit quietly, seething, munching on their battered jumbo sausages with scowls aimed at anywhere but each other.

Eventually, Pitbull breaks the silence.

"Stuck up prick."

"You said it," Jonno responds.

"Thinks he's better than us."

"They all do."

"Thinks 'cause he's some stuck-up middle-class dick, he has some kind of – of moral authority."

"Whatever that is, yep, agree."

Pitbull looks at Kacey. She sees in his eyes what he's thinking, and her grin grows.

No one knows Pitbull like Kacey does. She knows his real name is Jacob, she knows he likes watching men fuck her before they fuck him, and she knows how much he hates privileged bastards who think they are better than him.

Fortunately for Pitbull, it's the exact same kind of person that Jonno and Kacey hate too.

Pitbull has already decided the black eye wasn't enough, but he doesn't say anything. Not yet. He needs his plans to form first.

He wants to teach that guy a lesson.

And he wants to watch the guy's wife squeal.

And he wants them to suffer.

And he wants to derive pleasure from penetrating them with force they have never experienced.

He looks over his shoulder at Jonno. "You sure they are staying at that cottage?"

"They didn't have a car, it was the only place in miles they could walk to."

Pitbull nods. Looks out the mirror, resting his chin on his fist. Watches a mum, hair scraped back, second-hand jeans, giving her chips to her child. She sips some of her coke then hands that to her kid too. She's thinner than a woman should be. There is no shape to her body, like hunger has moulded it that way.

He huffs. Turns to Kacey.

"Shall we follow them?" Kacey asks.

"Aw, yes!" Jonno interjects. "And I got a great idea what we should do!"

Pitbull raises an eyebrow. Jonno rarely has actual great ideas. He's not really the thinking type.

"We just need to stop off to get Tibbles," Jonno says. "Trust me – it's going to be good."

Pitbull nods. Looks at Kacey. She's bites her lip. He can see her excitement, and this turns him on.

"Let's do this," he says, and shifts the car into gear.

As he reverses out of his parking space, Jonno cheers, and Kacey pumps the air.

It's going to be a hell of a night.

CHAPTER THIRTEEN

I DON'T TELL Lisa about what happened. I don't know why. Perhaps I feel ashamed. I do feel ashamed. But I feel just as ashamed for keeping it from her.

She is my wife. My love. My soulmate. I share everything with her.

I just can't bring myself to admitting – once again – that I am less of a man.

Am I less of a man? Is that what a man is – someone who can tell another man to fuck off?

If so, then I have never been a man.

I imagine a lot of people will tell me I was the bigger man for walking away. But I didn't walk away. I scarpered.

I didn't leave the situation because I was rising above it; I left because I was terrified.

"What's the matter?" Lisa asks, dipping a chip in the curry sauce. We're sat in the conservatory with the doors to the back garden open, listening to two birds fight on a tree branch.

The moonlight provides a vague light to the flowers that were so bright and colourful during the day, and beyond the garden we can see nothing but hills. But none of this seems so magic anymore. It's like watching a magician pull a rabbit out of a hat to see that the rabbit was in the bottom of the hat all along.

The perfect has lost its perfection, and I'm not quite sure how to bring it back.

"Oh, nothing," I lie. "My eye's just throbbing, is all. It hurts."

"Do you want another ice pack?"

"No, I'm just trying to forget about it."

"Okay."

I eat quickly and stay silent. I feel her watching me.

"These are good fish and chips," she says.

"They are."

"Have you thought about what you'd like to do tomorrow?"

"Not really."

"We could go for another walk."

"Could do."

She puts down her knife and fork and crosses her arms. "Michael, would you please just tell me what's going on?"

I sigh. "Nothing, I just… That guy scared me this morning."

She smiles sympathetically. I know she's being kind, but I feel like she's pitying me, and I don't like it. I want her to admire me, not feel sorry for me. I want to be her hero, not her project.

"The guy was a dick," she says.

"Yeah."

"And you shouldn't let a dick ruin our honeymoon."

Now it's my turn to put my cutlery down and fold my arms. "Okay, I'll just erase the experience from my memory then, shall I? As simple as that, is it?"

She doesn't reply. I hate the look on her face, and I hate that I caused it, so I quickly say, "Sorry, I know it's not your fault."

"It's not yours either. It's that guy's. That… Jonno's. He isn't worth–"

59

A loud noise interrupts her. We turn toward the sound. It came from the front garden, outside the living room, like something just hit the window.

"What was that?" she asks, standing, and I grab her hand and stop her.

"What?" she asks.

I don't know. I'm not sure why I stopped her.

"Nothing," I say, and she leaves the conservatory, and I follow. I feel suddenly cold. I rub my arms. They are shaking. Why am I always shaking?

I follow her through the kitchen and the hallway, and into the living room. There is something on the window. Lisa switches the light on.

It's blood.

On the window.

A dollop of blood, in a messy oval shape, with smears down the glass, like something has slid down it.

"Oh my God," she gasps, and edges toward it.

I stay behind her, knowing that chivalry means I should be the one leading her, but I'm too scared. I tell myself that chivalry and chauvinism are branches of the same tree, and that makes me feel better, like I'm empowering her, and not just being weak.

She reaches the window and looks out of it. Squinting. Sure that something is there, but not quite sure what it is.

"What?" I say.

She doesn't reply. Just stares.

"Lisa, what is it?"

"Have you got your phone?" she asks. I take it out of my pocket and give it to her. She turns the flashlight on and aims it out of the window, at the grass below.

Then she drops the phone, jumps back, and covers her mouth.

"What?"

She doesn't move.

"What is it?"

She turns away.

"Lisa?"

"Just – just look for yourself."

I walk slowly toward the window and pick up my phone. I shine it into the distance. I can't see anyone on the driveway. Then I walk to the window and point the light downwards to see what it was Lisa saw.

"Oh, bloody hell…"

It's the cat from earlier.

Its chest has been torn open.

It wriggles slightly. It's not dead yet. It's suffering.

"It's still alive," I mutter.

"What?" Lisa says, and rushes over to me. We both watch it writhe. We can hear it whine, though it's quiet. Lisa starts shifting her weight from one foot to the other, like she's getting ready for something.

I wish I hadn't told Lisa the cat was still alive.

I really, really wish I hadn't.

Because I know instantly that she's going to want to go outside and help it.

CHAPTER FOURTEEN

"GET SOME TOWELS."

I try to hold onto her hand, but she strides out of reach and I'm forced to let go.

"Lisa, please, don't–"

"I said get some towels."

I chase after her. "Please don't go out there."

"I'm not leaving the cat to die."

"But that Jonno guy might be there."

She tuts. "I can handle him, just get me some towels."

She opens the door and walks out of the cottage and disappears from view. I stare at the empty passageway, waiting for something terrible to happen, like Jonno rushing in and punching me or Pitbull running in with a knife or Kacey saying I came onto her again but – nothing. Nothing happens.

No one enters.

And all I can hear is my breathing. Quick. In, out, in, out. I think I can hear my heart thudding too.

"Where are those towels?" Lisa demands as she re-enters, the cat howling in her arms, its blood having already ruined her top.

I close the door behind her and turn the lock, then rush to the kitchen cupboards. I find plates, dishes, more plates – and then towels. I grab a few and follow Lisa to the dining room table, lay them out, and she places the cat on them.

Its mouth drops open. Its face droops. I can see its ribs. I don't know how Lisa thinks she'll be able to save it, but that's the thing about Lisa – she loves animals. Even when we both know this cat has minutes left, if that, she will persevere to the end.

She pulls its wound closed and places a towel on it, trying to stop the bleeding. Her arms are soaked in blood. I consider trying to find some gloves for her to wear, but it's already too late.

I try to block out the howling. It's awful. It's unlike any noise I've heard before. Desperation mixed with wailing mixed with agony, and I hate seeing something alive in so much pain.

Honestly, the best thing we can probably do now is put it out of its misery.

But we don't need to. Lisa is talking through all the possible places we could find a sewing kit, bemoaning how she didn't bring hers – as if stitches are going to help this cat – and its struggling becomes less. Its movement fades until its legs fall limp and its howling ends and its eyes are wide open, staring at us upside down, and I feel like I'm about to be sick.

I've never seen anything die before.

It's so final. The cat's eyes were moving, and now they aren't. It was suffering, and now it won't ever suffer again.

I put my hand on Lisa's shoulder. She covers her face with her bloody hands, not caring where she leaves red marks.

I try to think of something to say, but all I can come out with is, "I think we're going to have to replace those towels."

She scowls at me.

"I mean, sorry, I – I don't know why that's what I said. I just couldn't…"

I stop talking, feeling her frown burning my skin.

She turns out of my reach and marches away.

"Where are you going?" I ask.

"The bathroom. To clear this blood off me. Can you take it outside?"

"What?"

She pauses in the bathroom doorway. "The cat. I can't… Please, just take it back outside."

"You want me to go outside?"

"Oh, for Christ's sake, Michael, it's just outside, I'm sure you can manage."

"But what if whoever left the cat is there?"

"It was probably just a fox or something, I'm sure you'll be fine."

She goes into the bathroom, locks the door, and I'm left staring at it.

I really don't want to go outside. But this is a fragile moment. I don't want her to have to look at it. I want her to be able to wash away the blood and then, if we actually can, find a way to enjoy our honeymoon again.

I just don't feel safe on the drive.

But I don't want to upset Lisa.

I turn reluctantly to the cat; a contorted, bloody mess laying still on the table. I gag as I approach. The sight of it, so lifeless and distorted, sums up the finality of life in a way I don't wish to think about.

I cover its face and body with one of the towels so I no longer have to look at it, and use the other towels to wrap it up. Once done, I pick it up like a large cocoon and walk through the hallway.

I pause outside the bathroom, hoping to hear her. There are sounds of vigorous scrubbing, but no sounds of tears.

I unlock the door, take a deep breath, and reluctantly step outside.

It's so dark in the country. In the city, we'd be lit by a streetlamp wherever we go. Not here. Here, the driveway is black, and I can only see fuzzy outlines granted by the light of the moon.

I take the cat away from the house to the edge of the front garden and lay it down. I hope the elements won't destroy the body overnight. Then again, what are we going to do with it? Bury it? Burn it?

It probably has an owner.

I stand. Turn back to the house.

And I hear footsteps.

And I freeze

And those footsteps come closer.

And I turn around.

There is the outline of a man at the edge of the driveway, sauntering toward me with a cocky swagger.

I try to run, but my legs give way, and by the time I push myself back to my feet he's almost reached me.

"All right, mate," says a familiar voice. "Have you seen my cat?"

Light from the living room casts clarity on the features of his face, and I almost cry out in fear.

CHAPTER FIFTEEN

"WHAT ARE YOU DOING HERE?" I ask, and I hate the lack of conviction in my voice. I try to sound strong, but I just sound pathetic.

"I'm looking for my cat," Jonno replies. "You seen it?"

"This is private property." My lip trembles as I speak. "You need to leave."

He grins. "I don't think I need to go anywhere."

He steps toward me. I turn and run, sprinting back toward the house, resisting the wobble of my legs, throwing myself into the hallway then closing the door, locking it, bolting it, then rushing through to the living room where I left my phone.

Except my phone isn't there.

Where is my phone?

"Lisa!" I shout. "Lisa, call 999, that Jonno guy is back!"

She doesn't reply.

I lift the cushions and search under the sofas.

"Lisa!"

Still nothing. Is she still scrubbing in the bathroom?

I search by the fireplace, the lamp, the bookcase, behind

the television, then I find it. On the floor. The screen is smashed. It's unusable.

"Lisa, did you drop my phone?"

Still nothing.

I walk to the bathroom door. It's still closed. I gently knock on it.

"Lisa?"

Nothing.

"Lisa, please, I know you're mad, but we need to use your phone."

Still nothing.

I try the door. It opens. But Lisa's not in there. A blood-stained towel is on the floor and there's still bloody water in the sink, but she's not in here.

But her phone is.

I pick it up. The screen is smashed too. How did she drop both phones?

And how the hell are we going to call the police?

I leave the bathroom.

"Lisa?"

I pause and listen.

"Michael…" Her voice is weak and distant. It comes from the kitchen.

"Lisa?"

I walk through the hallway, then pause. The landline phone is gone. I swear, there was one on the little table in the corner, but now it's disappeared.

"Lisa, what's going on?"

I walk into the kitchen.

And I halt.

And my body stiffens.

"Lisa?"

She stands at the kitchen counter. Staring at me with wide

67

eyes. Her fingers fiddling. I'm not sure I've ever seen her look this scared.

"Lisa, are you–"

I step further into the kitchen, and I see *her*, sat on the kitchen side next to Lisa.

"Hi, Michael, is it?" she says.

It's the woman from the garage. The one who fixed our car. She wears a white vest and trousers and has tribal tattoos all the way up her arms and her neck.She also has a knife. A large one. I think it's a hunter's knife. The blade is long and curved, and someone would only have a knife like that if they intended to hurt someone.

"My name's Kacey," she says. "How are you?"

I can't speak. My voice doesn't come out.

I look at Lisa, who stares back, like she's on the verge of tears, and I wonder what Kacey has done to her while I was searching.

"I asked you a fucking question, Michael."

"I... I... Yeah... Fine..."

"Brilliant. Now why don't you sit down?"

"I can't–"

"Sit down, Michael, or I will gut your wife like Jonno did his cat."

I pull a seat out at the dining table and perch on the end of it.

"There! Perfect... Now we can begin."

CHAPTER SIXTEEN

I WANT to ask her what she wants. What she thinks she's doing. Who the hell she thinks she is to be in our safe space.

But I don't.

I just do what she says and sit at the dining table and stare at the knife.

"You ever watch someone fuck your wife, Michael?"

She stares at me and I'm not quite sure what I'm supposed to say to that question.

"No," I answer, my knees buckling, scared as to what might happen if I don't answer her.

"I mean, man or woman."

"No, I have not."

"You not into that at all then?"

"No."

"Ah, shame!" She slaps her knee in faux irritation. "Because me and my husband – Pitbull, you might have met him – we love it. We do. We fucking *love* it. And you two… You'd be just perfect."

"Please, we don't want anything from you, just take whatever you want and go."

She holds my eyes. Smirks. "Take whatever we want, huh?"

She looks at my wife in a way I really don't want her to. Like she's a snake about to swallow Lisa whole.

"You know what he means," Lisa says, and even though she's inches from that blade, she still has an air of authority to her voice – there's fear in it, but there's also resolve.

"Do I?" Kacey says, raising her eyebrows.

"I don't understand why you're doing this. We just want to enjoy our honeymoon, and if you would just let us, we'd–"

"Shut up."

Lisa stops talking.

"You talk too much," Kacey says, and if I had the guts, I'd be saying the same thing back to her.

"Fine," Lisa says. "I'll stop talking. And you can go."

"Can I?"

Kacey holds Lisa's eyes, her cocky leer meeting Lisa's determined gaze.

Kacey jumps off the kitchen side and, almost in the instant she does, Lisa reaches behind her and grabs a knife from the knife rack. A long, sharp one perfect for cutting meat.

She holds this out to Kacey.

Kacey doesn't even bother to raise her blade. She just watches Lisa's trembling arm.

But, trembling or not, she looks ready to use it.

"Just go," Lisa says. "Just go and we can forget all about this."

Kacey steps forward until the space between her breasts meets the tip of Lisa's knife.

"Go on," Kacey says. "Dig it in. That's the thing with knives, see – they ain't like guns. They aren't quick killers. They are slow killers, and they are always a gamble too – you can stab someone fifty times and they live, or you can stab them once in the right place and they will die. The question is, do you think you'd be able to kill me before I manage to raise my knife back at you?"

Lisa says nothing. Tears accumulate in her eyes. Her cheeks are red.

I could do something.

I should do something.

If I get another knife, it will be two on one.

Can I join Lisa before Kacey hurts her?

I must try something. I know I should. I don't have the guts, but I must find them, I must. So I stand. Ready myself. Clench my fists, and–

"Don't even think about it."

A deep, dark voice from behind me. I turn around and Pitbull stands there, grubby and bald – the ultimate alpha male.

He holds a hunter's knife, just like Kacey's, that he places right next to my throat.

"Tell your bitch to put that knife down," Pitbull says.

I turn to Lisa. I don't say anything. I don't need to. She throws the knife into the sink.

Jonno walks in. He bypasses me, giving me a wink as he does, and heads straight to Lisa. He takes her by the underside of the chin, lifts her to her tiptoes and puffs her mouth into a pout. He presses her against the kitchen side and presses his body against hers with enough pressure that she can feel every part of him.

"You pretty little thing," Jonno says. "They promised I could have you after they are done with him."

Have her after they are done with him?

What do they mean, have her after they are done with him?

Who's having *him*?

CHAPTER SEVENTEEN

PITBULL LEANS me over the dining table from behind and whispers in my ear, "If you struggle, we will split her open like the cat."

I turn my head and my fearful eyes meet hers, and I know I will not struggle. Even if I was going to dare – which, as I'm sure you can tell by now, I wouldn't – the threat keeps me securely where they want me, and I just pray that whatever he's going to do to me won't hurt that much.

Jonno tucks his hands around Lisa's waist from behind. He cuddles her like I did on our wedding day. She flinches as his erection presses against her hip. She can't move out of his grasp and remains stuck in this demented embrace.

Kacey strokes Lisa's face. Gives her a sarcastic pout. Puts the blade by her throat. Then looks at me, so I know what she's willing to do.

"What are you going to do to me?" I whimper.

I can feel Pitbull's grin.

I thought he'd hit me. Beat me to a pulp. Kick me until I bleed or until something is broken.

I did not expect him to reach around my front and

unbutton my belt.

"What are you doing?"

The tip of his blade presses between my buttocks and he whispers in my ear, "The more you ask, and the more you beg, the more it will hurt," and I vow to remain silent.

He undoes the waist of my trousers. Unzips my flies. Pulls my trousers to my ankles.

"Step out of them."

If I was looking back on this, I would rewrite my memory and pretend I didn't do everything he asked. I would stand up to him, and charge at those bastards threatening my life, and refuse to let Pitbull do whatever he wants to me.

As it is, I step out of my trousers and allow him to kick them away.

He takes hold of my briefs and pulls them down and my tiny little cock dangles like a worm in a bird's mouth.

I hear them laughing. I close my eyes.

When I open them, I can see Pitbull in the reflection of the window, and I can see his cock, and I can see him rubbing it, and I can't quite believe how big it is.

He places a hand on my left buttock. And my right. And he spreads my cheeks.

"What are you—"

His first thrust shuts me up instantly.

There's no lubricant. No moisture. It is dry, and he has to really shove his oversized phallus to get it in to such a tiny hole.

I scream on impact.

He pulls back and thrusts again, just as hard, and I cry out again.

When I was six, I had severe constipation for weeks then had to push a shit out so large it wouldn't flush. I've always remembered the pain of it, the agony as I pushed and it got stuck halfway out.

This is like that, except much, much worse.

"Please stop…"

Just as he promised, my begs make him thrust harder. The friction burns. I feel like I need to crap, but can't.

I look to the side. I see my wife staring back at me. Dismayed. Despaired. Tears spreading down her cheeks, violated by the man behind her, and laughed at by the woman who watches her husband violently fuck a helpless, wimpy man.

Something runs down my leg. At first, I think it's his cum. Then I realise it's blood.

Pitbull pulls back then pushes forward with all his body weight, and it reaches so far inside of me that it sends a feeling of fire up and down my rectum, and I think it's my prostate that feels like it's about to explode, I'm not sure, but I can't take it, I can't stand it anymore, and I almost pray for death and I beg for it to end then I see Lisa's face, and all I can do is weep – and weep silently, for fear that, if he hears me, he will make it hurt even more.

And it doesn't stop.

Each thrust makes me more tender and makes me hurt more and makes me feel like there are flames licking the inside of my arsehole.

He begins to grunt. He begins to go faster. It's almost over, I tell myself, it's almost over – except this is the worst part.

His grunts turn to screams and his screams turn to pleasure and his penis expands as he thrusts quicker and quicker and harder and harder and it becomes even bigger and explodes and I can't help but scream, cry out, unable to stop sound coming out of my mouth as it is the only way I can withstand the anguish.

And then he's done.

But he doesn't move out of me. Not yet.

I look down. There is a dribble of his cum mixed with a

pool of my blood.

He pulls out and I scream one last time.

And I fall to my knees.

It doesn't stop hurting just because he stops. The pain shoots up and down my anus, and there is more blood, so much blood, bright-red, dripping down my thigh and onto my foot.

I drop my head.

I can't look at my wife.

I'm too ashamed.

But I feel her watching me. She knows that I took this for her.

She knows I'd have probably taken it anyway, but it was my love that made me endure.

It is always my love that makes me endure.

"Michael…"

I hear her voice, soft like silk, distant yet close.

And I can't respond.

There's laughter. I don't know whose it is. Perhaps it's all of theirs, I don't know. But it's aimed at me.

All of it is aimed at me.

Because of what he did and how I look, on my knees, a grown man crying with blood trickling out of his backside.

Pitbull uses a tea towel to wipe my blood off his penis.

Then he throws the tea towel at me and it lands on my face and I don't even bother to remove it.

It's no more humiliation than I've already felt.

But the tea towel slithers down my chin and drops to the floor and they can see my face again.

And eventually their laughter dies down and I can just feel them watching me.

"Lovely, that was," Pitbull declares. "Nice and tight."

I close my eyes. I can't take anymore.

"Now let's see if your wife is just as tight, shall we?"

CHAPTER EIGHTEEN

"Don't."

It's a single syllable that's barely a grunt. A noise that summarises how pitiful I am.

Pitbull loves it. He turns to me, beaming, and asks, "What was that?"

I bow my head. Saying nothing, but wanting to say everything.

"I said, don't."

"You giving me instructions now?"

"No, I'm not, I, just… Please."

My insides throb. I meet Lisa's terrified stare with mine. Jonno still presses against her. Still treats her like an object to use and discard. As something these people not only want to play with, but are entitled to play with.

After all, an attractive woman is property of the world, not just herself.

"She doesn't deserve this," I plead.

"And you did?"

"No, that's not what I meant."

"And what did you mean?"

I huff. Feel myself getting desperate. Willing fate to intervene and make sure Lisa doesn't face the same destiny.

If they were willing to do that to me, then what are they willing to do to her?

"Just leave her. You've done it to me, just, please, not her..."

"Not her?" Pitbull points to Jonno and Kacey. "But what are they going to enjoy, eh?"

I close my eyes. Blood gathers on my ankles, semen dribbles down my inner thigh, and my anal cavity screams at me; but I make an offer in hope that they won't make Lisa endure the same pain I'm enduring. "Just have me again."

"You again?"

"Yes. Please."

"Sorry, mate," Jonno says. "Not my thing."

I open my eyes but stare at the floor.

"Look, if you–"

"I think we're done with this conversation now," Pitbull decides. "Jonno, as you were."

Jonno flicks his tongue against Lisa's earlobe, and it's something I've always done to her because it makes her tingle, but this ruins it, this turns an erogenous zone into an act of torture.

"Please, there must be–"

Pitbull grabs me by the throat and puts his face right next to mine, and he's snarling and his face is contorting and his lip is curling and he says, "Talk again and I'll cut her open," and leaves his knife by my throat to remind me of the constant threat, making the frailty of life apparent.

And so I don't talk again.

And I watch as Jonno shoves my wife to her knees. She makes eye contact with me and I wish she hadn't. Jonno kneels over her and moves her dress up her body and reveals her legs and her navel and her panties.

They are laced with red and are meant for me.

I turn my head away. I can't watch.

But I can't listen either.

Or be in the room.

I want to die.

In this moment, where I am almost shaking hands with death, with the blade beside my throat, I wish to die. If it means ending this suffering, ending the pain still firing up and down my rectum, and the sight of my wife having to endure this torture, for the pointless terror that has befallen us, then I wish to die.

And with this realisation I no longer fear the knife next to my neck.

I no longer worry for what it will do to me.

I am a coward. A chicken-shit. A wimp.

But this cowardly, chicken-shit wimp has had enough.

I have a black eye, a wounded ego, and a broken arsehole, and I am not going to let my feeble disposition hurt my wife any longer.

So I stare at the knife out of the corner of my eye.

I lift my hand, slowly.

Pitbull is watching Jonno. Enjoying the entertainment. He holds the knife, but doesn't pay attention to his threat, and I can grab it, I'm sure I can.

Lisa is crying and Jonno isn't even inside her yet – they are just marvelling at her beautiful, naked body – and my hand is rising, further and further, and I'm almost there, and I make my move.

I grab the knife.

I run past Pitbull and charge straight at the man accosting my wife, screaming as I raise the knife into the air.

CHAPTER NINETEEN

I MAY AS WELL SLIT my own throat.

Three of them, one of me.

Two of them with knives, one of me with a knife.

I'm not going to get very far, running at them, screaming, waving my arms around like I'm trying to scare a cat out of my garden.

Jonno hasn't even flinched. He just smiles. He fucking smiles, finding my attempt at standing up for myself – probably the first time I've attempted it in my life – amusing. Almost endearing, in fact. Like I was a baby taking his first steps and falling over.

Pitbull's boots pound on the kitchen tiles behind me and I turn and I swing the knife, scraping his chunky thigh as he steps out of the way.

Pitbull looks angry, and it's made me even more scared; worried that he now wants to hurt me more.

"Get off her!" I shout, turning back to Jonno.

Jonno stands. Holds his knife by his waist. Kacey steps forward also, twirling her large blade.

Lisa looks up at me, then back to her body, her skin

already bruised, and what hurts me most is not the humiliation she suffers from her nudity, but the wounded expression that destroys her dignity. Lisa is a strong, fierce, independent woman, and she does not let anyone talk down to her, or make her feel like she's not worthy enough of the same promotion or attention or opportunities as a man.

And they have stripped that from her.

She no longer looks like the dominant, beautifully intimidating figure she so often is – but looks like a vulnerable child scared of the world.

She meets my eyes, and she sees Pitbull charging toward my back, and I just give her one simple instruction: "Run."

She shakes her head. She won't leave without me.

Dammit, Lisa, now's not the time.

Pitbull knocks me in the back, sending me to my knees, and sending the knife flying across the room.

"Now! Go!"

"I am not–"

"Just go!"

She hesitates. Reluctant. Caught between two awful decisions, and I wish she would just listen to me.

"Please," I whisper, and this seems to do it, as she pushes herself to her feet and runs just as Jonno's knife lands in my back, and I have never felt pain like it.

She pauses at the doors to the garden, half in the kitchen looking back, half escaping.

"Go!"

Pitbull looks at her and, almost to show off how vindictive he is, he pulls me up by my hair and sends his large, beefy fist into my jaw. I feel it dislocate as I fall to my belly.

I try to tell Lisa to go again, but I can't anymore. Whether it's the blood in my mouth or the dizziness in my mind, speech seems to have left me.

In fact, I don't even know if she is still at the door. I'm too focussed on the pain; the way I can't close my mouth anymore, how my chin seems to be stuck too far to the right.

Is that my tooth on the floor?

Pitbull grabs my hair again – at least, I assume it's Pitbull – and he lifts my head until I am at waist height, then, with all the force his might can muster, he brings my head down, colliding it with the kitchen tiles, and it feels like my head is made of bricks. I've gone cross-eyed, I think. There's a constant scream going from the front to the back of my head, then back again.

"Ooh, my turn, my turn!"

Who's that?

It's a woman.

Something sharp thrusts into my spine and my legs twitch.

"Let's take him into the garden, make sure she can see us."

They drag my body into the garden, where nothing but a fence separates the cottage from the fields that go on, and on, and on.

"There she is!"

She? Are they talking about Lisa?

I try to lift my head, but it won't budge. Then Pitbull has my hair again and he's dragging me across the garden by it, and I can feel the agony of each individual strand.

He places my head through the gap in the fence and rests my neck against the wooden beam.

His boot lifts, blocking the moon, and he brings it down, colliding it with the back of my skull, and my neck breaks.

And I can't move.

I'm still alive, but I can't move.

All I can do is stare at the grass and feel my body empty itself of life. The pain is immense and I'm not breathing and my heart has either stopped or slowed down and everything feels a little more hazy.

I try to focus my final thoughts on something nice, but all I can think is *I am dying I am dying I am dying* as if it changes anything.

I wasn't ready to die. No one ever is. But this is how it is.

My body is shaking. I can't control it. It feels like I am having a seizure, but it's probably just a few minor twitches.

I picture Lisa's face on the grass. Looking up at me, smiling that smile.

I never did deserve her, did I?

A guy like me doesn't get a woman like that. It was all wrong. It just didn't fit. I should be with some nasty, unattractive nerd with body odour. Not with a knockout like that.

But I was with her.

And now I'm not, I guess.

I'm starting to get cold now. Everything is growing darker. I think it's time.

There really is no painless way to die, is there?

I close my eyes.

Lisa holds my hand and tells me she'll stay with me. I know it's not really her, but I don't care. I go to thank her, but I don't seem to have the thought power to imagine me doing such a thing.

That's when the final bout of pain comes, and it ends.

And I die, with the woman I love beside me, telling me it's all going to be okay.

LISA'S STORY

CHAPTER TWENTY

I MAKE it across two fields until I look back. In the distance, I see the light of the kitchen. I see Pitbull, Jonno and Kacey leaving the garden and pursuing me.

And I see my husband's lifeless body slump over the lowest panel of the fence.

I fall to my knees, then push myself up again.

I have to keep going.

But Michael…

I squint. Try to be sure. Is he really dead? Could he be unconscious?

His neck is pointing the wrong way. He's not moving.

Oh, God, Michael…

I have to get up. I have to run.

They are chasing me. They are quick, and my body is torn between collapsing and crying, and I need to think carefully about what to do next.

I think of what they will do to me when they get me and what they did to Michael, and it convinces me to get up and run, to move my aching legs, to ignore the despair and use the adrenaline.

I glance back, hoping that Michael's body will move and he will stand up and everything will be okay.

He doesn't move, he doesn't stand up, and everything *will not* be okay.

He's dead.

He's dead.

Oh God, he's dead.

Just stop thinking it. Stop letting the image go round and round my mind like a demented carousel, it's not going to help, I just have to get away.

They leap over the fence and into the adjacent field.

I reach the next fence and climb over it, falling in the mud, my bare skin clothed in dirt, and push myself up again and tell myself to run, run, just run, just keeping running.

Michael is dead.

Just move those legs.

They killed him.

Just keep them going.

You won't ever see your husband again.

I reach a field that will take me out of view of the cottage. I look over my shoulder again, just one glance back, hoping he will leap to his feet and wave.

He's dead, they killed him, and you will never see him again.

They are so much closer now than they were.

I run toward the moon, no idea where I am aiming for – there are no houses, no phone boxes, nothing. There is a country road in the distance, and more hills beyond that; I have nowhere to go.

Then I see it.

My God, I see it.

A light. Two of them. Beams. A car on the road.

It's a few fields over and it's going to pass but I can get to it in time, I'm sure I can, I know I can.

So I sprint harder, my legs moving and my arms moving

and my body panting and I do not look back – I will not look back – I will keep going, aiming at the headlights as they approach, and I will not look to see how much they are gaining on me.

I leap over the next fence. Fall. Pick myself up. Will myself to keep going. I run so hard my lungs struggle and legs ache and my head hurts and I have a stitch, but I don't care. I just keep going.

I leap over the fence and into the final field.

The headlights approach, and I become terrified that I'll miss them.

I run across the field, and this one's muddier, and I slide a few times and my bare feet squelch and I don't care, I do not care, I just have to make it, I have to make it, I have to, I have to–

"Help!" I scream as I run onto the road as the car turns the corner and, for a moment, I think it's not going to stop and it's going to run into me.

But it does stop. In fact, it screeches to a halt, and the door opens and I'm worried that, after all this, it's going to be one of them.

But it's not. It's an old lady, with grey, curly hair and veiny hands.

"Are you okay, dear?" she asks, and I have never been happier to see another human being in my life.

CHAPTER TWENTY-ONE

HER NAME IS AGATHA. She looks like a toe after getting out of the bath – small, shrivelled, and mole-like. She doesn't have a phone, and she doesn't quite understand what's happened. Her mind isn't all there. She knows she needs to take me to the police – who she says are twenty minutes away, but will be longer at the speed she drives – and she knows I've been hurt, but aside from that, she doesn't quite grasp the severity of what's happened.

Then again, do I?

"…This really is most strange…"

What has just happened?

An hour ago, we were eating fish and chips. So why aren't we eating fish and chips now?

"…To be accosted in such a manner…"

I'm on my honeymoon with my husband, so why aren't I with him?

"…I mean, in my day we didn't let ourselves get so muddy…"

I tune her out and wrap the towel she gave me tighter around my body, which is suddenly cold. She wanted me to clean myself off before I got into the car, and seemed quite upset when I wouldn't, and found it rude that I kept turning back to look in the field.

Thankfully, she finally stopped moaning and drove.

"…Why you youngsters wish to run around without your clothes anyway, I don't know…"

I look at her. She's a small, fragile woman, with large glasses perched on the end of her nose. Her arms shake – Parkinson's, maybe?

In the drinks holder between us is a leaflet about the early signs of dementia.

"…Just trying to drive home and you get mud all over my seat…"

I turn away from her. She doesn't matter. She's driving slowly, but at least she's driving. I need to think. I need to understand what's happening. I need to…

They killed Michael.

No, don't think it.

Just pretend it didn't happen. Until I'm safe. Until I'm with the police, and we can go back and see if he's okay. I saw the body, but he may have been unconscious, he could have still been alive, he could…

Pitbull snapped his neck.

Yes, but I was far away, and I was running, I didn't see it well enough to know.

You saw it just fine.

Okay, well, then maybe it didn't kill him. Maybe it's just a broken neck: I broke my arm when I was a kid, and it's fine now.

This isn't useful, Lisa.

But he could still be alive. I know it. I feel it in my gut.

Your gut also told you Frome would be the perfect place for your honeymoon.

Shut up!

Please, just shut up, I can't take it!

I scrunch up my eyes. Cover my face. Shake my head.

This isn't happening this isn't happening this isn't happening this isn't happening.

I cry. Weep. My body convulses with every sob, and I hate being the cliché. The crying woman in a horror book – don't you just hate that?

I always skip this part – the part where the woman has to cry. Where she doesn't shout; she screams or screeches. Where she can't handle the pain, and her crying becomes wailing. And she has to be scantily clad and pathetic, just like every other female victim in horror.

But what do you want from me?

I am not your Final Girl. I am not your Monstrous Feminine. I am not just a trope.

The Final Girl has strength to fight. I barely have enough strength to live.

"Careful, dear, you're getting mud on the door."

She's right. I've left a muddy elbow print on the arm rest. I take my hand away and rest it on my lap.

I catch sight of my reflection in the window; I'm red-eyed and red-faced. The mascara I wore for our romantic evening is smudged. The lingerie I wore for Michael is ripped and torn, somewhere back in the cottage.

As is my husband.

I wipe my eyes. This isn't the right time to let those thoughts get the better of me. I'm not safe. I have to focus. I keep looking to see where I am.

We turn from the small country road onto a slightly wider country road. There are houses in the distance. Not many, but at least it means there are people.

A pair of headlights approach us from behind. Their high beams are on, and they are gaining on us quickly.

"Oh dear, they seem to be going awfully fast…"

I turn around. The headlights are right behind the car; so close they are almost colliding with the bumper. She is driving really slowly, but this is unnecessary; she's very old, and these people should be more patient.

They flash their lights.

"Maybe I should pull over."

I squint, trying to see past the bright light so I can see what they look like. I'm about to agree that she should pull over when the high beams go off momentarily, and I catch a glimpse of the face behind the steering wheel.

"Do not pull over," I say.

"Really, it's the best thing to do."

"No! Do not pull over!"

"I am the driver, young lady."

"You don't understand – they are the ones who attacked me!"

"Who attacked you?"

I punch the seat. I know it doesn't help. She just frowns and begins to slow the car down.

So I beg.

"Please don't stop... Please... You don't understand..."

"We will get you where you need to be in good time, but I don't want to have an accident–"

"They will *kill* you!"

"Now, there's no need to threaten me."

The headlights get closer to the car and almost collide.

The woman begins to indicate.

"No!" I say, and I throw my leg over the gearstick and press down on the accelerator. The car revs and speeds up and Agatha looks at me, furious.

"Get off!" she says, hitting me with her weak hands. "Get off now!"

The car almost goes into a hedge so I grab the steering wheel and turn it back toward the road. I try to keep the car under control despite her persistently hitting my arm.

The jeep gets even closer and nudges the bumper.

"We need to go faster!"

"Get off!"

"Please!"

"I am pulling over and you can get out–"

She doesn't have the chance to pull over as the jeep nudges the bumper with more force. The car spins and Agatha panics and I grab the steering wheel, twisting it to the side, then back again, trying to steady the car.

I manage, and we stay on the road.

Behind us, the headlights get smaller, and the jeep drops further back, and I think he's going to leave us alone.

But he isn't.

He's just getting a good run up.

"No!" I cry out as the jeep speeds up and gains on us and it's going too fast and it collides with the car, sending it spinning to the left, to the right, and I try and straighten it with the steering wheel but it keeps moving left, right, and I have no control over it.

The car veers down the verge and collides with a hedge.

Agatha is hyperventilating.

I climb over her, put the car into reverse and hit the gas.

It won't move. It's stuck.

And the door to the jeep is opening.

CHAPTER TWENTY-TWO

"Come on!"

I push harder and harder and the engine gets louder and louder but still, the car does not move. It remains nestled in a small ditch, the bonnet in a bush, the back wheels in the air.

A figure leaves the jeep and approaches through the darkness. His face is hidden by the night, but his figure is unmistakable; I can see the outline of the thick, well-built body – it's Pitbull.

"Look what you've done!" Agatha cries out, tears in her eyes. Her arms shake. She can't look at me.

Pitbull's face appears at the window. He signals for us to wind it down and I grab Agatha's arm so she cannot open the window.

"Do not wind it down," I urge Agatha. "He's going to hurt us."

"Please, help me!" Agatha calls to Pitbull. "This woman has accosted me!"

"Agatha, please…"

Pitbull tries the car door. Finds it to be unlocked. He opens it and looks past me at Agatha, smiling like a concerned citizen would.

"Is everything all right, M'am?"

"No!" she moans. "This woman assaulted me!"

"Why don't you step outside," he says to me. "And let this woman out."

"Please…" I beg him. "Please, don't do this…"

"You've been in a crash, and she's elderly. We need to make sure she's okay."

"Why are you doing this?"

"Get out of the car – *now.*"

I turn back to Agatha, who looks at me with such fear that I almost think I am the evil one.

Pitbull doesn't wait any longer. He grabs my arm, pulls me out with ease, and throws me to the road. The solid ground hurts my knees. The cold makes me shiver. Crusted mud falls off my thighs and onto to the gravel.

When I look up, Pitbull has helped Agatha out of the car. He does so with care, holding her hand delicately and helping her to her feet, constantly reassuring her that it's going to be okay.

Just as she goes to thank him, he grabs the back of her head, takes a clump of her grey, curly hair in his fist, and rams her forehead hard into her car bonnet. Blood runs in a straight line down her nose then down her chin.

I scream and I turn and I run.

I want to help the lady, I really do, but there's nothing I can do.

I flinch as I hear the impact of her head against the car again, and after the third strike I glance over my shoulder to see Pitbull drop her. Her body lays in a heap on the ground. She isn't moving.

Pitbull smirks at me. Winks. Waves. Then returns to his jeep.

I run harder.

I will my legs to move.

They are so tired, and I don't think I can go much longer, but it is my life I am fighting for, and I tell myself just to keep going, please keep going.

And I force them, despite the aching, despite the agony, despite the terror, to keep fighting for my life.

I hear the engine behind me, and at first I am worried they are going to run me down, but they don't. Instead, they play with me. Driving inches from my backside. Speeding toward me and slowing down. Nudging me so I stumble.

I can hear them laughing through their open windows as I keep sprinting. They aren't even trying to kill me. They are trying to torment me. Like a lion playing with its food.

What is wrong with these people?

These people...

These *monsters*...

These *monstrous people* who killed Michael.

Oh, God, they killed him...

These people killed Michael...

The bumper of the car nudges me again and I fall to my knees and push myself back up. I see a road turning to the right and I wait until we're about to pass the junction, then I quickly take it. The jeep carries on and screeches to a halt, and it stalls before having to reverse, which gives me a bit of time.

Then I see them. Up ahead. A row of houses. Old, Tudor houses. With lights on inside.

I see a person walk past a window. A man with grey hair.

Oh my God, there's a person there... He could call the police and he could lock me in his house and I could be safe...

I hear them running behind me.

I do not look back. I sprint toward the houses, just running, concentrating on nothing else, fighting the fatigue, and I reach the first house.

I fall on the welcome mat and my blood drips onto the W.

I push myself up and stretch my arm toward the doorbell and to go press it – but something grabs my arm.

It's Jonno.

I scream and he places a hand over my mouth and muffles my cries. I kick and thrash and do everything I can, flailing every limb in every direction, making myself as hard to hold still as possible, and I feel Jonno scoop me up and into the air, gripping tighter and tighter to avoid dropping me.

Then I see Kacey approaching me. With a needle.

I scream again, and I try biting his fingers, but it's his palm that covers my mouth. I make it as hard as I can for Kacey to stick the needle into my body, and I kick out, and I thrash, then Pitbull grabs my legs and holds them still.

I can't speak. I can't move. So I use my eyes, meeting Kacey's with mine, and plead, woman to woman, *please don't do this, please don't, please...*

She shoves the needle in my arm. I feel a little prick, and whatever was in that syringe enters my bloodstream.

My body loses its energy. My limbs weaken. My mind becomes hazy.

My eyes close.

And as they do, I realise that my chance is gone, and I'm probably going to die.

CHAPTER TWENTY-THREE

WHEN I COME AROUND, it's light. Sun shines through the window. I'm in a bedroom. Kacey sits on the bed. I'm lying on it.

"Hey you," she says.

My skin pricks. I look down. I'm naked. My nipples are erect from the cold. My breasts fall to the side. There is already semen dribbling from my vagina.

I try moving my body and find that my wrists and my ankles are fastened to the corners of the bed.

I scream.

"It's no use."

I scream anyway.

Kacey doesn't say anything else about it. She lets me get it out of my system, like a child with too much energy.

She finishes tightening a handcuff around my wrist, then smiles dotingly, like she cares, and places an affectionate hand on my cheek.

"My darling," she says. "Just relax. You may as well – you're not going anywhere."

"Why are you doing this?"

"Me? Oh, I like to watch. That's all."

"And how would you like it if I did this to you?"

She laughs. "Pitbull's done this to me many times."

"What?"

"I have to say, I love it. The thrills. The unknown. He ties me up and watches his friends fuck me. It turns him on to see me being enjoyed by so many men."

"What?"

"My advice would be to just enjoy it."

Kacey takes a spoon and a yoghurt from a bedside table.

"Open wide," she tells me.

"What?"

"You need your energy. Now open wide."

She puts the spoon to my lips. I keep them shut.

"Are you going to be difficult?" Kacey asks.

"You can fuck off if you think you're putting anything in my mouth."

She laughs.

"My darling, that's not where we'll be putting it."

She laughs some more.

"Honestly," she says, "you're lucky. Pitbull's good. So is Jonno. You won't be disappointed."

I feel helpless. I feel tears. This woman is mental. She's offering me to these men like she's doing me a favour.

"Now, eat," she says, putting the spoon next to my mouth.

I refuse to open it.

"Fine, if that's how you want to do it."

With her other hand, she grabs my nipple. She twists it. It hurts. She holds the spoon by my mouth, and she tugs my nipple again, grabbing it harder and twisting it until it can't twist anymore and, finally, I open my mouth, and I let her put a spoonful of strawberry yoghurt on my tongue.

"There," Kacey says. "Isn't it better when we work together?"

She feeds me the rest of the yoghurt. I reluctantly let her, glaring at her the entire time even though she doesn't seem to notice. She's like a clueless child, unaware that all the other kids hate her.

"I don't want to do this," I tell her.

"Do what?"

"Any of it! You seem to think it's something I'll enjoy, these people, they ki – they ki…"

I can't say it.

I can't say what they did to Michael.

I can't even acknowledge it.

Kacey strokes my face again. She leans down and kisses me, softly, then stands up and heads for the door.

"Don't go," I whimper, and I don't know why I want her to stay.

She just smiles at me and exits the room and I'm left here, bound to the bed in the cold, with yoghurt smeared on my lips.

I test the restraints. I pull at them, harder and harder, but they won't yield, and the headboard barely moves, and neither does the end of the bed that the ankle restraints are fixed to.

I'm stuck here.

I try screaming again. There's a window, perhaps someone could be walking past the house and hear me.

My voice becomes hoarse and, eventually, I give up.

I don't know how much time passes. It could be minutes, or hours, it's hard to tell, but, eventually, Jonno enters.

He grins at me but says nothing. He starts undressing. His vest, his grubby jeans, his shit-stained underwear, until his cock wilts out. There's a wart beside his foreskin and a mole on his testicles.

"Please…"

My begging only seems to spur him on, so I say nothing.

I just prepare myself. Mentally. And I pretend to be somewhere else.

Anywhere else.

We're back at home. We've just bought our house. Michael collects the keys but doesn't go in yet, not until I'm home from work; it's something we do together.

We walk from room to room, amazed at how big it is, aware that it will feel so much smaller once we've unpacked.

It's a week later and I've just dislocated my thumb and forefinger and Michael opens every door for me. I tell him that I can still open doors but he insists on me doing nothing until it's healed. He says he broke a leg once, and it hasn't been the same since. After something has broken or dislocated once, it can break really easily a second time.

We walk around the garden. Talk about getting a dog, or a cat. About kids. We want two. Twins, maybe. They run in both our families.

Days later, we are almost unpacked and we are watching the television. I'm watching the England football match and Michael is pretending to care. I laugh at how this is typically the other way around; the man's supposed to force the woman to watch the football.

We go out for drinks and we celebrate, and Jonno is grunting over me harder and exploding inside of me and we toast, Michael and I, at finally being home owners.

Jonno takes himself out of me then penetrates me with a douche, ensuring to clear as much out as he can.

And I lay there.

And he leaves

And I don't bother crying, because there's no point anymore.

Pitbull comes in shortly after, and the process is repeated and this time I'm thinking about Michael's proposal, a year ago in the Yorkshire Moors. We went walking in the rain whilst on holiday. We always loved the rain. My mum always used to say there's no such thing as bad weather, just bad clothing, and we get drenched but that made it all the nicer when we arrived home that evening and sat by the fire.

Pitbull goes and Jonno comes back in later on.

Kacey brings food and, whilst she doesn't fuck me, she inspects me, shining a flashlight on my breasts and telling me to "spread your legs wide" so she can "inspect your cunt."

She goes and Pitbull returns and Jonno returns after, then it's dark again and I've pissed the bed and the house is silent.

I wait and I wait until it's late enough to be sure that no one is awake.

I hope that they are done with me for the day.

And I decide that I can sneak past them.

But first I have to get out of this. Release myself from bondage.

So I take a deep breath.

Let it out.

And I look at my fingers.

The handcuffs are pretty tight, but Michael was right in what he said, you know. Back when we moved in together, and my thumb and forefinger were dislocated.

Once something has dislocated once, it really is quite easy to break it a second time.

CHAPTER TWENTY-FOUR

THE ADRENALINE WON'T NUMB it completely.

This is going to hurt.

It hurt the first time I broke my fingers. I was standing on a chair at work, trying to physically demonstrate the different levels of social class used in *Blood Brothers* to my students, and I fell off, putting my hand out to break my fall and landing on my fingers, two of which ended up dislocated. It hurt, and I was unable to stop myself from crying in front of students.

There's no one to see me cry now.

I'm not sure if I'm even capable of crying anymore.

People cry. I am no longer a person.

I am a naked sack, used and discarded until I'll be used again. I have different men's body liquids congealed on my leg. My vagina is sore. My skin is cold. Humiliation left hours ago – now I'm just empty.

But I have a chance.

I stare at my thumb. I can still see a slight mark from where I broke it before. That's where I need to aim it.

The question is, how on earth do I dislocate my thumb with my wrists and ankles bound? I need to hit it against the headboard with force, and it's going to be tough to get enough force without being able to put my body weight behind it.

But the thumb is fragile. It's not long since it mended. All I need to do is to shove it against the headboard with a little bit of strength, and at an angle that will force it to bend in a way that will allow me to pull my hand out of the handcuff.

And I have to make no noise. Not a sound.

I stare at my fingers, willing myself to do it.

Please, Lisa.

Please, just do it.

Please, just get on with it, while they are probably asleep, while I have a chance.

Before they come back in the morning and continue using me as their human dumpster.

But still, I don't move. The memory of the pain of breaking my fingers is still too vivid. I don't know if I can do this.

You have to, Lisa.

I know I do, but I can't...

Fine, then just stay here and be used until they decide to kill you.

They might not kill me.

*They killed Michael; they are going to kill you too.*Don't say that. Please, just don't say that.

The image of Michael lying over the bottom fence, his eyes wide but empty, his body slumped – it haunts me. It's a constant reminder; this is how it ended for him, and how it will end for me.

"Right," I say, unaware of making the decision to speak. "Come on."

I loosen my wrist. Try to avoid the handcuffs jangling. Pull on them a little, just to make sure they won't give; just to make sure I have no choice. And I aim my thumb at the headboard at a skewwhiff angle. An angle I know will dislocate it should I give it enough force.

"Come on Lisa, come on, just do this, come on..."

I pause. Take a deep breath. Prepare myself for the pain, and shove my thumb against the headboard.

It hurts. But it doesn't dislocate. And it makes an almighty clatter.

I pause, waiting, listening to see if anyone has heard it, staring at the door in anticipation of someone bursting in, angry, ready to abuse me for the impudence.

I don't move. Not yet. I keep staring.

But no one comes.

I breathe a sigh of relief, then remember what I have to do.

I rotate my hand at the headboard and shove it again.

It just hurts, but doesn't dislocate it. I need to put more force into it. I can't be afraid to make noise.

I'm going to have to make noise.

I just have to pray they don't hear it.

Right. Here goes. This is it.

I pull my hand back as far as the handcuff will let me – which isn't far – and I pause, and I breathe, and I shove my thumb hard against the headboard.

I barely hear the clatter, I am too focussed on the pain. I catch my breath, barely able to think about anything but the agony.

It doesn't ease off.

It keeps on and on and on and I just wait for someone to walk in and find me here, biting my lip, holding back the tears, trying not to scream from the anguish.

But no one comes in.

And my thumb is dislocated.

I allow myself a moment. Try to calm my panting down to steady breaths.

I stare at my thumb, pointing in the wrong direction – but the right direction for me to pull my hand out of the restraint.

I pull my arm and it slithers through the handcuff, the bumps of the restraint rubbing against the tenderness of the thumb, and I try not to moan as the pain shoots up and down my hand as I release it from its bondage.

The ankle restraints are not fixed with handcuffs, but with leather straps, and they are easily loosened, and I am able to pull my legs out.

I hadn't, however, thought about the handcuff on my right wrist.

I look around. Searching for something. A hairpin, a knife, whatever – just *something*.

But the room is empty of everything but me and the bed.

I examine the headboard my arm is fastened to. I pull on it a little. It wobbles. Could I pull it free?

A sharp pain fires up my left arm, a reminder of how much my dislocated thumb hurts.

I pull on the headboard. I put a leg against the wall and pull harder.

It won't budge.

And then I hear it.

From down the hallway.

Footsteps. Heading this way.

"Shit!"

I quickly shove my feet back through the ankle restraints.

Then I turn to the handcuff I'd just freed myself from. I don't hesitate. With tears in my eyes, I shove my hand back through, rubbing the metal against the tender bone until it's back in.

The door creaks open.

Jonno's smug face appears. Same white vest, grey tracksuit bottoms, sweaty scalp.

"Hello there," he says. "I was hoping you'd be awake."

I scan his body. Searching for something I could use, if only I could get hold of it.

From his trouser pocket, I see it. The tip poking out.

The key.

CHAPTER TWENTY-FIVE

HE MOVES to the bottom of the bed, and he's about to crawl over me and enter me and plough me and I can't let that happen.

"Please, don't," I say, but it only makes him smirk as he ignores me.

"Haven't you had enough of being down there?" I ask.

He looks puzzled.

"Please, I'm too sore, why don't you... why don't you let me use my mouth?"

He looks at me, slightly bemused.

"Fuck off," he says, jokingly, not quite able to believe that I'm making the suggestion.

"I'm being serious."

"How do I know you're not just going to bite it?"

It's a good question. "Because I saw what you did to my husband. And I know that you will kill me."

I flinch as the image reappears my mind.

"If you so much as give a hint of hurting me," he tells me, "I will shove my knife up your cunt."

I nod. "I just can't take anymore down there... I need to

rest it... Please, I'll use my mouth, I promise I won't hurt you."

He looks at me. Pauses. He's deciding, and his decision will change everything.

Finally, with a lecherous grin I am becoming too accustomed to, he walks to the head of the bed.

He places his knees either side of my neck. He pulls his trousers down his thighs. It dangles helplessly in front of me, and I can see a bit of smegma around his foreskin.

I could bite it off.

I could.

But what then?

That's not the plan.

I take a deep breath, ignore how much his pubes stink of piss, and place my mouth around it. He's cold and I'm warm and he looks to the ceiling and closes his eyes.

I'm good at this. I know I am. I know I can distract him well enough.

I start by licking the tip. Running my tongue around his foreskin. Then I put it in my mouth. All of it, until I choke. Guys seem to like that. Michael always liked that.

I look up at him whilst I audibly gag for his benefit.

His eyes are closed. He's in ecstasy. He's moaning.

I go faster, then slower; I can't let him cum yet.

I pull my hand through the handcuff and try not to scream or flinch or howl as I put myself through the pain all over again.

I go a little harder instead of screaming. He moans again, and he's enjoying it too much to realise I have a hand loose.

I put a loose finger into Jonno's pocket.

"Oh, fuck, yeah..."

He starts to open his eyes. Shit. I go faster, and I moan myself, like I'm enjoying it, like I'm not trying to make myself go numb, like I'm not choking a little on his precum.

I push the key under the pillow. Nudge the pillow a little,

until it's over it. Then, once again, I brace myself for the pain and shove my hand back through the restraint, unable to help myself from whining. He thinks this is part of my enjoyment and he moans himself and I have what I need, and it's time to finish this.

I go faster. His hands grab the back of my head, scrunching my hair in his fists, and he shoves himself harder and harder into my mouth, all the way until I'm gagging over and over, and the cum fires at the back of my throat and I try not to throw up.

When he finishes, he puts his hands on my neck and tells me to swallow it.

I open my mouth to show that I have.

"You are a surprise, ain't you?" he says. "Maybe next time I'll go for your mouth again."

He steps away. Pulls up his trackies. Smiles at me. Looks me up and down, from head to foot, from the urine stains to the cum stains. Then he laughs.

"Wow," he says. "You really are pathetic, ain't you?"

I glare at him.

"Oh, give me evils all you want – you are so helpless you just sucked my dick to save your cunt."

I ignore that he's right. I ignore that he's taunting me. I have the key, and I need him to leave.

Keep your mouth shut; the key is all that matters.

With another chuckle he leaves the room and shuts the door. I hear another door open and lock, then I hear the faint tinkle of him urinating.

I drag my hand back through the restraint and yelp and feel the sting and pull my ankles out and shove the pillow aside with my head. I pick up the key with my skewwhiff fingers and shove it in the lock beside my right wrist. I turn it and the handcuff opens, and my wrist is loose, and I am free.

I am free!

Not yet.

No. Okay. What do I do?

Get out.

Yes. Quickly.

Now, go!

I step out of the room, tread quietly across the hallway, and creep down the stairs.

It is pitch black outside. Night-time in the country is the blackest night-time there is.

If I run, they'll catch me.

I need a vehicle.

The jeep is outside. Where are the keys?

A toilet flushes upstairs. The bathroom door opens. Footsteps approach the empty bedroom.

"What the fuck?"

Shit.

I need to find those keys.

I search the kitchen. The cupboard. The drawers. Beneath the leftover pizza boxes and around the empty beer cans.

"Pitbull! Kacey! She's loose!"

Through the living room. On the windowsill. Under the sofa cushions. Behind the 65-inch flatscreen TV. Under the beer cans on the coffee table.

Footsteps pound down the stairs.

I am shaking. Stop it. Just hurry.

Through to the hallway. The front door is in sight, but I don't use it yet. I search the pockets of the coats hanging from the coatrack. Under the dirty shoe rack. In the shoes.

Jonno's shadow approaches me.

Pitbull and Kacey appear at the top of the stairs.

I open the front door, about to accept that I have no vehicle and I just need to run – then I see them.

Attached to the house keys in the lock of the front door.

I open the door as Jonno charges at me and my legs ache

but I run, sprint, harder, toward the jeep, hearing feet behind me.

I open the door to the jeep, throw myself in, then lock the doors.

Jonno's body slams against the window and he tries to get in, but he is unable.

"You bitch!"

I ignore him. He can call me all the names he wants, it doesn't matter.

He launches a fist at the driver's window. Again, and again.

I shove the key in the ignition, turn it, and the engine comes to life.

I see Pitbull and Kacey running toward the jeep in the rear-view mirror.

Jonno's fist pounds against the window, cracking it on the third attempt.

I put the jeep into gear.

He keeps pounding against the crack until his fist smashes the window and he grabs me and I hit the accelerator. The car accelerates and his hand is around my neck but I speed up, and it's too fast for him, and he drops off, and I speed along the country road, not caring how fast I go, just speeding.

They disappear in the rear-view mirror.

I have escaped.

No, don't get ahead of myself.

Just drive.

And so I do, expecting every moment to see them in the mirror, to see headlights approaching.

I see nothing.

Even after hours, when the petrol light comes on, I see nothing.

I have escaped.

Oh my God, I have escaped.

And they have no idea what they have created.

CHAPTER TWENTY-SIX

Pitbull looks at Jonno.

Jonno looks back like a scared little boy.

"What the fuck have you done?"

Jonno says nothing. This makes it worse.

"You fucking imbecile!" Pitbull charges at him, pushing him, shoving him back. "You fucking idiot! What have you done?"

Jonno doesn't fight back, and Kacey doesn't try to stop her husband.

Jonno feels for his pocket. He trembles. The keys aren't there.

Pitbull, still in the underwear he was sleeping in when abruptly awoken, launches a fist at Jonno's face and lands it against his cheek. Jonno falls to the floor and Pitbull kicks him in the face, knocks him onto his front, and still this tough guy doesn't fight back.

Because he knows he deserves it.

They all know he deserves it.

"What the fuck is wrong with you!" Pitbull continues to scream. "What did you do? What *the fuck* did you do?"

"I'm sorry..."

"You're sorry? You're fucking sorry? She'll go to the police, you fucking idiot – she'll go to the police, and then what? Our DNA is inside of her! You think that a jury will have any doubt it was *us*?"

Jonno covers his face. He knows he's screwed up. Pitbull knows it too. Kacey, rubbing her body as the cool night air pricks her skin, fears that she may lose her husband's freedom along with her own.

"Fuck!" Pitbull roars, then turns away, one hand on his hip and the other running through his hair. He launches himself at Jonno again, throwing another punch and another, until Jonno's blood is on his fist.

Kacey puts a hand on his shoulder. It makes him stop beating the idiot. He expects her to say something comforting, but she doesn't.

There is nothing she can say.

They are fucked.

And they spend the next few days cleaning up Michael's body, getting their facts straight, and preparing their story ready for when they get a knock on the door from the filth.

Pitbull makes sure his affairs are in order, just in case. He ensures his business is also in Kacey's name and that the money is there for her if she's able to escape charges – and he blanks Jonno.

Jonno stops coming round to the store. In fact, Jonno stops speaking to Pitbull altogether.

After a few weeks pass, however, they start to wonder.

Where are the police? Are they investigating? Perhaps following them, waiting to see if they are led to Michael's body?

Michael's body is buried in multiple places across the Somerset countryside; they'd never find it.

But another few weeks go by, and the police still do not arrive.

This makes Pitbull more unsettled, as he doesn't understand why.

Did the police not believe her?

How could they not, with the state she was in?

Then again, they live in a world where the victim is often blamed rather than believed – *thank God* – and it may well work in his favour.

After two months, Pitbull begins to relax a little.

Maybe the roz aren't coming, after all.

He carries on working. He drinks at the local pub. He fucks his wife, and whatever other party they ask to join.

His life resumes routine, and he grows tentatively confident that they have gotten away with it.

Little does he know that there is a reason the police haven't knocked on the door.

Little does he know there is a reason Lisa never reports what happened.

Little does he know that prison would be a luxury compared to the true justice that will be inflicted on him.

You see, Lisa could go to the police – then what? The semen would be theirs, yes, but she would have to prove it wasn't consensual sex. She'd have to take the stand and be figuratively raped by their lawyers, with her full sexual past analysed and picked apart. They'd bring up her ex-boyfriend, who is now in prison, and use that to claim she probably wants revenge on *men* for what that convict did to her.

And Pitbull likes to involve other parties during sex with his wife – how can they prove that wasn't simply the case here?

Yes, there are marks on Lisa's wrists and ankles. But so what? She likes it rough. Pitbull's lawyer could get an ex-boyfriend of hers to testify to that. She never objected to being tied up every now and then – of course, she only likes to be tied up by someone she loves and trusts, but that won't matter to a lawyer, will it?

And even if, after the long, laborious, traumatic trial, Pitbull, Jonno and Kacey are convicted, then what?

Ten years in a comfortable prison cell and they'll be out again.

But what about Michael? Does she owe it to him to tell the police what happened?

Then again, what would be the use? Would a few decades in a prison cell be sufficient punishment for what they did to him?

No, Lisa does not go to the police.

Why would she?

There is far better justice in this world than what society provides.

And Pitbull, Jonno and Kacey are about to find that out.

PART III
THE SHITBAGS

JONNO'S STORY

CHAPTER TWENTY-SEVEN

THERE'S a lot of fit birds out in town today, enjoying the sun, wearing their short skirts and vests and getting their legs and tits out. They know what they are doing, flaunting their bodies like that – each and every one of them is screaming out for it.

My ex once tried to tell me that birds are humans too. Fuck that. I never met a woman who's anything more than a hole to aim at.

"Can I help you?" one woman asks as she walks past me. She has large hoop earrings and tits the size of watermelons.

"Just enjoying the view, love."

She tuts and turns away and I love it – that moment – that feeling – when they think they have some moral high ground because I let my dick do the thinking.

If they had a dick, they'd think with it too.

"Jonathan?" a man asks , poking his head out of the door to the job centre. He wears a suit, and he sounds like a school teacher.

"It's Jonno."

He offers his hand. I sigh and I shake it and he leads me in, past the numerous unemployed people searching for jobs on computers and phones, and into his cubicle.

I smirk as I sit down. This guy doesn't even have an office.

"Okay," the man says, "let me just get your file up."

He clicks a few buttons and looks at his computer screen. I slouch down in my chair, run my hands over my freshly shaved head, then shove them into the pockets of my tracksuit bottoms.

"Ah, here we go. Jonathan Tyler. Right, let's begin." He turns to me and smiles. "My name is Clark, it's good to see you. How has the jobhunting been going?"

I shrug my shoulders.

"Have you filled in many applications?"

"I can't fill in applications."

"Why not?"

"I'm itilerant."

"Do you mean illiterate?"

"Dunno. I can't, like, read too well, and I can't fill them out."

"And have you asked for any help?"

I shrug again.

"Right, okay." Clark clicks his mouse a few times and stares at the screen. I'm not sure what he's looking at. Probably porn. "See, it says here that you have been unemployed for almost two years now. We like to get people back to work within a few months, if possible, rather than–"

"Look, can I have my dole money or not?"

He looks at me like teachers used to look at me. Like he's better than me. Like having to deal with me is the worst part of his day. I want to punch him for it, but I can't – I need my dole money.

"We don't just hand it out," Clark says. "We like to make sure you are, in fact, trying as hard as you can to get work. I mean, it says here that you sent off some job applications independently a few months ago."

"I had help from a mate."

"And can that friend help you again?"

I glare at Clark. I don't know what he wants from me.

"Nah, we fell out."

"And are you able to make up?"

I huff. This is none of this bloke's sodding business.

"I don't think so," I say.

"Have you tried calling this friend?"

Yes. I've tried calling him.

I've tried calling both him and his wife.

But Pitbull doesn't want to talk to me.

Nor does Kacey.

They say I fucked up. That it's my fault. But that bitch is probably dead – it's been months and no police have showed up or nothing. So I don't get why they don't just forgive me.

It used to be that, any time the dole people gave me a hard time, Pitbull gave me a bit of work to show that I was trying.

Now he gives me nothing.

And I have spent the last few months drinking beers on my own all day.

No one wants to talk to me.

No one.

No fucking one.

"Look, can we just get this sorted, yeah?"

"I really think that you need to show–"

"I don't fucking care!" I lean forward. "You giving this to me or not?"

"Mr Tyler, please do not threaten me."

"Threaten you? Nah, a threat is something people do when they are all talk. I'm perfectly happy to follow through."

"Please, I do not–"

"You have no idea what I can do, you bullish twat. Now

sort my dole money out, or I will follow you home and break your family's faces. Yeah?"

He looks torn – somewhere between asking for help and giving in.

So I hold his stare. Like a dog.

The toughest dog in the pack always holds eye contact the longest. It's how they show that they don't take any shit.

And that's what I am.

A tough dog.

With giant tough-dog-balls.

And this guy is just the little bitch who lays on their back when I walk past.

"Rightyo then," Clark finally says. "Let's get this sorted."

I grin and lean back. Look around while he types on the computer. Some bird is sat down at the cubicle opposite with a small skirt and her legs crossed and I can almost see her knickers.

"Okay, you are sorted for the next two months. But we will need to see–"

"Cheers."

I stand. I don't need a lecture, I need a piss.

So I leave.

To go home.

To my cheap little council house.

Alone.

CHAPTER TWENTY-EIGHT

FIVE MINUTES of staring at the television and I'm done. There's fuck all on. So I head to the pub, and three hours later I'm sat at the bar on my sixth pint and my head is starting to spin.

"Hey," I say to the barman as he passes. "Hey, yo, yeah, you."

He smiles and I can tell he doesn't want to talk to me but I'm too battered to give a shit.

"Do I know you?"

"No, I don't think so."

"Yeah no I think I, er, wait – what?"

"Pardon?"

"I forgot what we was saying…"

He walks away.

"Hey, don't, er…"

I turn around. A woman is at the bar. She's asking for shots. She's wearing a dress. It's got flowers on it. If I lean back enough while she's leaning over the bar I can just about trace my gaze up the top of her thigh and see her–

"Er, excuse me?"

I sit back up. Blink away the fuzziness.

"Can I help you?" she asks.

I grin. Oh yeah you can help me, you can help, you can, wait, what…

Hang on…

Huh?

"What was the question?" I ask. Then burp.

"Oh my God, you are revolting."

"Hey! I got feelings too, I may…" I catch a whiff of my vest. I've been wearing it for days. Girl's got a point, to be fair.

"Fine, I may stink," I continue, "but you…"

"Can I get you anything else?" the barman asks her.

"Nothing," I say. "I'm fine."

They both ignore me and she orders pays for her shots and if I lean forward, instead of leaning back, I can just about make out her bra. She's got tiny little tits. I like them big, but I'm not fussy.

"Can you mind your own business?" she snaps.

"What?"

"You are a fucking pervert!"

"Woah, hey, I…"

I look around. Where's Pitbull gone? Wasn't he here?

No, wait, he wasn't.

He doesn't like me anymore.

It makes me laugh, and it turns into a cackle, which turns into hysterics, and I realise I'm drooling down my chin.

"Oh my God, you are so disgusting."

"Yeah, and you are a slut."

"Oh, original. Well done."

She takes her shots and fucks off and to hell with her – she wasn't that fit anyway.

"Barman, another!"

"Are you sure you should have anymore?"

"Hey, I am an adult, I can figure it out for, I can – erm, yeah."

"Right, well this is the last one, then I'm cutting you off."

"I'll cut you off!"

He pours my pint. Asks for money. I dig into my pocket and pull out a load of coins. I throw them onto the bar and he stares at me as I count out the £3.20 I owe him.

It leaves me with just a few pennies left.

Looks like that's the end of this month's dole money.

The next thing I know, a pint of beer has appeared next to me and I'm not quite sure how it got there.

I turn around. Scan the pub. There's a woman on her own, reading a book. She looks lonely. Maybe I should keep her company. Maybe she's here on her own because she wants a man to go chat her up.

"Hey!"

She doesn't look up. I'm sure she heard me, though. Everyone else is looking at me.

"Hey, you!"

She glances nervously at me.

"Hello!"

She waves a hand then goes back to her book.

"You're on your own too!"

She doesn't look up.

"Hey, I'm talking to you!"

She still doesn't look up.

"You're being rude! I'm talking to you!"

"Okay, mate, that's enough," the barman says.

"What? I'm trying to be nice. She's on her own, I'm on my own, why don't we, just like, I don't know…"

"I think she's on her own by choice, buddy. Probably doesn't want your attention."

"Oh, fuck off!" I turn back to the woman. "Hey! Don't you want my – my, er… my – my attensho…"

"Right, that's enough, time to go."

"What?"

"I said, time to go."

"No, it's not. You're open for another few hours, I know you are."

"Yeah, but not for you."

"Fuck off, I'm not going anywhere!"

The barman walks out from behind the bar and he's beside me and he's putting a hand on my back.

"Get your fucking hand off me."

"Get out, mate. Get out or I'll chuck you out."

"Hey! I am not–"

He grabs my arms and hooks them behind my back. I try to fight, but everything just gets too dizzy, and I don't know where I am, and he pushes me out of the door and shoves me onto a pile of stubbed-out cigarettes and I hear everyone inside cheer.

I look up at him from my place on the floor.

"Fuck you," I say. "You have no idea who you've just fucked with."

The barman snorts, says, "Sure," and returns inside.

I stand. Shout something else at him – I'm not sure what, it's just stuff coming out of my mouth – and I walk along the street, stumbling from one closed shop to another, using a bin to help me along, and why is it so dark at night?

I throw up, though I'm not aware of throwing up. It just happens, and the next thing I know I'm on the floor and my knees are in it.

I push myself to my feet. Cross the road. Into a field. I'll take the fields home.

I'm sure the fields lead me home.

Don't they?

I'm not really sure what happens after that. The next thing I know, it's sunny, and I'm opening my eyes, and I'm in the field, and I'm lying in a pile of cow shit.

CHAPTER TWENTY-NINE

I TRUDGE HOME, stinking like manure, and have a quick shower. I can't afford that much hot water, so it has to be quick. I can still smell a bit of shit on me afterwards, but a change of clothes seems to help.

I walk into the kitchen, rubbing my head, and check the time. It's gone eleven in the morning. I open the fridge. Three cans of supermarket own-brand lager are left. I consider having a cup of tea instead, but I don't have any milk. Or tea bags. Or a kettle.

Beer it is.

Behind my house are two rows of garages facing each other. They are covered in graffiti and weeds. Kids usually play football or smoke dope between them. I'm lucky enough that my council house backs onto them, so I have a backdoor that leads directly to my garage. I take my beer, and my mobile phone, and walk through the backdoor to where I find my 2002 Ford Fiesta in the same shitty state I left it. Maybe I'll carry on fixing it this morning.

Then again, what's the point? Even when it's fixed, I can't afford the road tax, or the insurance.

Fuck it, I'll drive without.

What are they going to do? Put me in prison?

Been there. Done that. And it was a piece of piss. Maybe I'll bump into some old friends while I'm there. Would be good to catch up.

Then again, for a driving offence, I'll probably end up in a low category prison, which would be shit. My GBH conviction for nutting a Millwall fan put me in a category B. I don't want to end up in a prison with all the nonces.

I take the phone. Dial Ma's number. Put it to my ear and let it ring.

She answers eventually.

"Hello?"

"Hey, Ma."

"Who is this?"

"Jonno."

"Jonno?"

"Your son."

"Oh, Jonathan."

"It's Jonno, Ma."

"Right."

There is a silence between us for several seconds.

"What do you want?" she asks.

"Was just wondering if you fancy having me around?"

"I'm busy today."

"Tomorrow then? Or Sunday? You doing a roast?"

"I'm busy, Jonathan."

"Jonno."

"Whatever."

I sigh. Stare at the car. I once drove all the way to Scotland in it. Pitbull and I partied in Glasgow. I woke up in the driver's seat next morning and drove us back home again. We stopped at the services and had a full English breakfast. We had the windows down and the stereo at full volume and I drove ninety down the motorway for the entire journey.

Now the piece of shit is nothing but glorified pieces of scrap.

"Next week then?" I ask.

"I'm doing things with Trevor."

Trevor. Ah. Of course. The latest boyfriend.

He's a dickhead, like the rest of them.

"What about–"

"I've got to go now, Jonathan, Trevor is calling me."

"It's Jonno."

"Goodbye."

The line goes dead.

I stand still, waiting for her to speak, like the repetitive dial tone is lying to me, and she's still there. But she ain't. And I'm just stood here, holding a phone with no one on the other end.

I fucking hate Trevor. I hate that guy. I hate them all.

I launch the phone across the room. It hits the far wall and the case comes off and the battery falls out. I don't give a fuck. I have no one to call anyway, so I go into the garage and think about working on the car.

I grab the hook from the rope pulley I have fixed to the beams in the roof of the garage, pull it down, and attach it to the front of the car. Pitbull was going to throw the pulley out, as it was old, and it was rusty, and they were getting better machines to lift cars with. I said I'd have it. I love it. I use it to lift my car into the air and look at the bottom of the engine. Sometimes, I imagine how great it would be to get someone to look under my car, then take the hook off and let it drop on their head.

I decide I can't be bothered to work on my car anymore. I'm not in the mood. So I go for a walk. It starts to rain, but I don't care. If anything, it cleans my clothes so I don't have to waste water on cleaning them myself.

With my hands in my pockets and my hood up I stride, not quite sure where I'm going, through the estates and past dog walkers and couples and old friends meeting up. Everyone has someone but me.

I end up at the train station. I like it here. A few years ago, I actually managed to pick up a bird here, so it's probably the best place for me to go.

And I see one. A little chubby, but whatever. Sat on a bench, staring at her phone, her legs crossed. She wears a leather jacket, a low-cut top, and light blue jeans. From the look on her face, she could do with cheering up.

I sit next to her.

"Hi," I say.

She forces a smile.

"What you doing?" I ask.

She pulls a face. "Just waiting for a train."

"Where you going?"

She frowns. "I don't really want to tell you."

"I ain't going to follow you or nothing. Unless you want me too." I grin at her. She doesn't grin back. I don't care. Her jeans are tight and her hair is pretty and I can see the crack between her breasts, and why would she dress like this if she wasn't after attention?

"You all right?" says some bloke as he approaches. Wearing a long, fancy coat. Hair gelled to the side. Sounds like a teacher. "Is this guy bothering you, honey?"

I laugh.

"What?" he asks.

"You. *Is this guy bothering you, honey?* Who the fuck are you?"

"I'm her husband, that's who."

I snort. "Married birds are the easiest. She's bored with you, mate. Bet I could have her bent over the bonnet of my car by the end of the day."

He laughs. "I think the most shocking thing about what you've said is the idea that you can actually afford a car."

I stand. Charge toward him. Get in his face. "You got a fucking problem?"

He doesn't back away. He doesn't cower. He just stands there, smiling at me. It's patronising, the way he looks at me. Like I'm a kid. I hate it, and I want to fuck him up.

"I just want to sit with my wife without you here, that is all."

He walks past me and sits beside his wife. He puts an arm around her. They kiss, and they prolong their kiss, as if to mock me. As if to shove it in my face.

"Come on then," I say.

The guy takes out his phone, stares at the screen, and ignores me.

"Come on then!"

He kisses his wife again. They close their eyes and don't pay me a bit of attention. It infuriates me. There is nothing I hate more than being ignored.

Everyone ignores me. Ma. Pitbull. Even fucking Trevor. I will *not* take being ignored!

"I said fucking *come on then!*"

He doesn't stop kissing her.

It's useless. He ain't going to pay attention.

And I feel myself crying.

What a fucking pussy.

I turn, march away, not wanting them to see me.

I *hate* being ignored.

I hate it!

But who gives a fuck?

There's no one who cares. No one at all.

My best mate ain't bothered anymore.

I can't even get attention from some chubby bitch at the train station.

I'm alone. Always alone. And I can't even afford to eat, because I wasted it all on beer.

I charge home, getting drenched as I do. The morning sun is gone. Thunder clouds loom overhead.

Maybe I should kill myself. That'd teach them.

Teach who?

It wouldn't teach anyone, because no one would care. I could hang myself in the garage and no one would find me until I started to smell worse than this estate already smells – which would take a while.

I approach the house.

I'll drink.

That's what I'll do.

Drink until I can't stay conscious, then I won't feel anything.

I take out my keys.

And I stop.

There's someone sat against my front door.

A woman.

I'm confused, at first. I think it's Kacey. I get hopeful. But it's not.

It's not her at all.

I slow down. Walk toward her.

And I recognise her.

And my heart quickens. I sweat. My entire body tenses.

Then she says exactly what I did not expect her to say.

"Oh my God, I'm so glad you're back!" Lisa claims. "I've been waiting for you."

Is she bringing the police?

Is this a trick?

What's going on?

She rushes up to me and I get ready to fight – but she doesn't seem angry at all. She seems happy. She throws her arms around me and squeezes me and *fuck* it feels good to feel the touch of another human.

Especially a woman.

Her arms wrapped around me make me feel warm, and I feel special, and I feel loved.

I am so pathetic.

One hug from her and suddenly I'm happy again.

She looks up at me. She looks so small and dainty. She goes onto her tiptoes to reach my lips, and places hers against mine, and I let her, and we kiss.

"God, I'm so glad you're here," she says, and she goes back to hugging me, and we are getting drenched in the rain but I don't care.

I hug her back.

"I've been so desperate to see you," she says. "I haven't stopped thinking about you. Have you been thinking about me?"

She looks up at me again. Her face is covered in rain. Her hair is soaked. But she looks stunning.

"Yes," I tell her. I don't know if it's the truth or not, but I want to believe it.

"Can we go in?" she asks. "I'm getting really wet."

"Okay."

I let her in, and I fetch her some towels, and I don't know what's going on, I really don't – but she hasn't brought the filth. And she really seems pleased to see me.

Maybe she enjoyed it. Maybe she liked us being rough with her, and she's come back for more. Some birds are into that kind of stuff, ain't they?

Either way, I feel a sudden need to protect her. To keep her close. Like I love her already, just for her showing affection toward me.

Fuck, it feels good to have a woman touch me again.

I lock the front door behind us.

CHAPTER THIRTY

I ASK her if she wants a beer and she takes my hands, looks me in the eyes, and says, "No alcohol. We don't need it."

And I believe her.

I don't know why. It's something in her eyes. A sincerity, maybe. There's kindness. I've never seen that in a person before.

At least, not toward me.

"I'll make us a cup of tea," she says. "How about that?"

I go to tell her that I don't have any tea, but she's brought a bag and she takes teabags and milk out of it.

She starts opening cupboards, trying to find the cups. She isn't bothered that I don't have a kettle, as she boils water on the stove with a pan. Then she looks at me and chuckles, and I become self-conscious about how I'm standing here awkwardly.

"You can sit down, you know."

I can. So I do. At the small table that only sits two, but normally sits one.

A few minutes later, she puts a cup of tea in front of me.

"So how have you been?" she says, and I'm suddenly confused.

Am I stupid? Is this a trick or something?

Why would she be here, being nice to me?

We attacked her, didn't we?

"I don't get it," I say, and I hope I don't offend her.

She just smiles sweetly. "Get what?"

"What you're doing."

"Yes. It is all a bit bizarre, I must admit. Even I was quite hesitant about coming here."

"But... why?"

"Why what?"

"Why ain't you gone to the police?"

She doesn't answer straight away. She stares at her mug, her hand nestled around its warmth, but she doesn't drink it.

She shifts position. Crosses her legs the other way. Then talks.

"I suppose that's the question, isn't it?" she says. "Why didn't I just go straight to the police..."

I nod. She thinks more. I wait for an answer.

"Well, I was going to. As soon as I got into the jeep, and I'd put a few miles between me and the house, my next thought was to go to the police station. But there was just... *something...* holding me back. I don't know, it must sound crazy."

"It don't sound crazy. But I still don't get it."

"I just couldn't stop thinking about you, Jonno. At first, I thought it was anger. That I resented you. That I couldn't stop thinking of you because I hated you so much. Then I realised – it wasn't hate. In fact, the moments you were inside of me... they were the only moments I've felt alive in a long, long time."

"But, your husband... We killed–"

"We? You did nothing. It was Pitbull. And if anything, it freed me. It means there is no other man in the way of... *us.*"

It still feels weird. We hurt her. Me included.

But even so, it makes sense.

Some women like to be tied up, don't they? Some women fantasise about some manly bloke – like myself – breaking down the door to their house and forcing them to do all those things they won't let their husband do.

I gave her the fantasy, and now she's obsessed with me.

I could pity her if she weren't so good-looking.

"You could say something," she tells me. "I mean, I'm sat here, spilling my heart out, and I don't even know if you feel the same."

"Well, it's hard to say…"

"Oh, don't be coy."

She leans toward me and takes my hands in hers. It's the most someone has been willing to touch me in a long time, and the touch of her skin almost makes my lip quiver.

"I know it's not instant," she says. "I know this is out of the blue and, well, you're probably not going to feel the way I feel straight away. And if you don't think you will, then please, tell me, and I'll go. But, if you think there is, maybe, just maybe, a tiny smidge of a chance that you think you could love me, then… Please, put me out of my misery."

I grin. Make her wait. I've never thought about loving someone. They are just words I use to get a bird to fuck me.

But could I?

It would be one hell of a story when people ask how we met!

"I guess," I finally say.

Her face lights up. She rushes from her chair and onto her knees beside mine, and she wraps her arms around my waist and hugs me. Her face is inches from my crotch. She's squeezing me tightly, and I give in and hold her back, and we stay like this, just holding each other, and I've never done this.

I've never even cuddled with a woman.

It feels good. It feels like I'm loved. Like someone may actually want me around.

To hell with Pitbull and Kacey.

Fuck you, Ma and Trevor.

Piss off, that barman and that couple on the train station and everyone else who shuns me from their world – I have someone now.

I am not alone anymore.

And I feel like crying – man tears – but I don't, because I'm not a pansy.

"Can we go to bed now?" she asks.

"Really?"

"Yes. I want you to hold me. And I want to touch your naked body with mine… if you are ready, that is. I don't want to rush anything."

"Yeah, no, safe, we can do that, yeah…"

She stands and smiles. "Do you mind if I have a shower first? You go get yourself ready in the bedroom."

"Go for it."

She stands and practically dances across the room. She pauses at the stairs and turns back to me.

"I'm really glad I came back," she says. "I was worried, but now I know I did the right thing."

She takes another look at me and she rushes upstairs. Minutes later, the shower is on, and I can still smell her on me.

She smells like happiness.

Like company.

And I rush up the stairs, taking off my clothes as I do, barely able to contain my excitement.

CHAPTER THIRTY-ONE

I STRIP off and give my armpits a sniff. Not great. I've been saving the water and only showering every few days, and up until now it hasn't mattered. No one else is ever around to smell me.

Fuck it, if she likes me that much, then she'll put up with a bit of BO.

So I lie on the bed in nothing but white socks and I try to get myself hard. I don't want it all small and dangly when she comes out of the bathroom – I want it rock solid and waiting for her.

The shower stops running.

Shit. I'm as limp as a dead flower.

I rub and I rub and I rub and then – oh, and then my friends – she emerges, and I don't have to rub to get myself hard anymore.

She is wearing nothing but a red laced bra and a red laced thong. It's barely there. And she's shaved. Shit, she's shaved.

I'm the luckiest son-of-a-bitch alive.

She smiles timidly, and she looks young and vulnerable and naive, deceptively innocent – childish in a way you just want to wreck. She saunters toward me, swaying her hips, and her thighs are curved just right, and her hair flows over her shoulders, and she goes to the end of the bed and climbs onto her hands and knees. Slowly, she crawls up me, over me, her hair brushing my cock in a way that is undoubtedly intentional, and she reaches my chest. She runs her tongue from my navel to my nipple, and she runs her hand up my thigh and over my balls and past my dick – the fucking tease – and up my chest. She reaches my face and she kisses me, and it's intense, passionate in the way I've only seen Pitbull and Kacey kiss.

And, for the first time in my life, sex is better than porn.

I go to take off her bra and I fumble. I can't get the clasps. She does it for me and says nothing. Her tits are small and perky. I slap one. It wobbles. It makes her giggle. I fucking love it.

I go to touch her, and she pushes my hand away and says, "I want you in my mouth. Like before…"

I don't disagree. That was the best blowjob I've ever had.

She moves off the bed, and goes to her knees, and turns me around so I'm sat on the edge, and she licks my thigh, and licks my balls, and licks my shaft, then puts the whole thing in her mouth until she gags.

I lean my head back and look to the ceiling and close my eyes and just enjoy it. Fuck it, why not? I earned this.

She goes quicker and harder.

She even uses a little teeth, just enough to gently rub me.

I'm not sure I like it, but fine.

She gags and I get harder and she uses a bit of teeth again.

It puts me off.

Then she carries on and she rubs me harder and I'm close, and I'm close, and there are those bloody teeth again.

"Watch the–"

I'm not able to finish.

And I'm not sure what's going on at first.

There was a little teeth, then a lot, then suddenly all I can feel is teeth sinking into me, going further and further and I'm screaming and it hurts like holy hell and I'm screaming more and she's still doing it.

I try to shake her off, but that just makes it worse – every movement hurts, makes her teeth sink further in, and I can do nothing but stay completely still.

"What the fuck are you doing!"

She looks up at me. Meets my eyes. There is no pleasant, innocent look to her anymore – this look is demented. Deranged. As fucked-up a look as I've ever seen in a woman.

"Get off! Get off now!"

She doesn't.

In fact, she clamps her teeth down harder.

I swing a fist and land it in the side of her head, but it forces her teeth to bite harder and so I don't punch her again and I don't know what to do, I can't wriggle, I can't hit her, I can't get her off in any way.

"Please! Please fucking stop!"

But she doesn't stop and she keeps staring and it's agony now, absolute fucking agony, and her teeth have penetrated the flesh and the muscle and are sinking in further.

"Fucking stop you fucking psycho!"

I'm crying and it's pathetic but I don't care right now I really don't care it just hurts it fucking hurts and she won't stop she won't stop why won't she fucking stop!

"Please…" I beg. "Please… Please stop…"

I'm sweating and the pain is penetrating my whole body and there's blood pouring down her chin and my leg and she's sinking her teeth in harder.

I put my fingers in her jaw and try and pry her teeth apart, but it's like trying to open a clamp that's been wound shut but I keep trying, and my fingers slip on the blood and there's too much of it for me to get a good grip.

Then she slams her teeth together.

And I fall to the floor and I writhe and I wriggle and the blood is dribbling over the bed and over the floor and she stands. Looks over me. Like a frenzied goddess looking down on its pathetic subject.

"What the fuck have you done!"

The pain is too immense for me to really understand what's going on, but then I look down and I see it.

And I don't believe it.

Not at first.

I chopped a tree down a few weeks ago, and all that was left was a stump, and it's like that except there's more blood.

She opens her mouth.

There it is.

I scream something but I'm not sure what.

And she spits it out like a mouthful of toothpaste, and it lands on my face and slides like a slug, leaving a trail of blood across my cheek.

"You fucking bitch!"

I stand up and charge at her but something is in my neck.

It's a needle.

I don't know where it came from but she had it, and she's pressing on it, and it's sending something into my bloodstream that makes me fall onto my back.

I think I'm going to pass out, but I don't.

And I try to get up.

But I can't.

In fact, I can't move at all.

My eyes can. They can wander around, surveying the room, analysing the bloody face of that psychotic whore – but my body won't move. My muscles are limp.

And my dick is gone.

She crouches beside me and pinches my cheek.

"In case you don't realise," she says, "that was a paralytic. Also called a neuromuscular blocking agent, normally used for surgery – except you've had a much higher dose, and I don't think it's going to wear off."

I try to say something back but all that comes out is noise and drool.

"You can't speak, honey, remember?"

She stands. Smiles.

"Now, let's begin."

CHAPTER THIRTY-TWO

SHE DRAGS me across the room and to the stairs. She has to stop and wipe sweat from her forehead. I'm a big fucker, and she's a little girl. But I don't put anything past this bitch.

She's ready to do whatever she has to.

After a brief pause, she takes my leg and drags me down the steps. My head bounces off each one, leaving me with a pounding headache.

I can't move. I can't speak. I can't even flinch.

Yet the pain is immense, a constant stinging, a painful emptiness where my greatest weapon used to be.

I almost don't care what she's going to do to me now. What is the point of living without a cock?

But it's still up there. In the bedroom. They can reattach it, can't they? I've heard of it happening. There was that woman in America a few decades ago who chopped of her husband's dick and he had it reattached. The guy even went on to do porn.

I'd love to do porn.

She just needs to save it for me, to get me to a hospital, but

I know she won't. I can't even beg her to. I try talking but all that comes out is more dribble and disgruntled noises.

When she pauses at the bottom of the stairs to take another breath, she looks at me and smiles. She licks her lips, like she's having a naughty thought, then she holds her leg in the air, and swipes her ankle down upon my gaping wound.

I howl without being able to howl.

I scream without being able to do more than gurgle.

I call her a bitch and tell her I'll kill her and say that she's a fucking whore without being able to do more than think it.

She laughs at me. I don't blame her. I'm pathetic.

I try asking what she's going to do to me, but my saliva forms a bubble and I almost choke on it.

It's starting to go numb now. The stump between my legs, that is. Just like the rest of my body, it's starting to lose all feeling, and I don't know if that's because of the pain reaching its limit or whatever she injected into me.

Yet every time I look down and see nothing there, I feel the pain, and it fires through my empty body.

She grabs my leg and pulls me across the floor. She keeps heaving and sweating and panting and pausing, but she gets me across the kitchen, to the backdoor, and into the garage.

She drags me toward my old, battered Ford Fiesta, and for a moment I think she's going to run me over with it, but she doesn't. Instead, she grabs some rope and begins tying it around my ankles.

She's good, too. She knows how to tie a knot. She goes around each ankle individually, then around both, until there is no way I could escape it even if I was able to move.

Then she attaches my ankles to the hook on the rope pulley. The small, rusty one Pitbull gave to me.

She turns to me.

Smiles.

And she uses her entire body weight to pull on the rope,

and the hook slowly raises me into the air. Until my arse is above my head. Then my back drags across the dusty ground, followed by my neck, then my head, and it raises me higher and higher until I am dangling upside down. My arms flop below my head and I am as helpless as a kitten.

She goes to her knees and grins at me. I can still smell her. Her tits are upside down but still perfect. Her skin is still smooth. Even though I hang here, humiliated, naked, and dickless, I still want her, and I have never hated myself as much as I do right now.

"I'll be right back," she says and gives me a playful slap on the cheek.

She returns to the house. I hope that someone will hear me as I scream, but I can't, it's just noise; just elongated grunts and chokes.

When she returns moments later, she is fully clothed again, and she has a banana with her. She closes the garage door, sits on the bonnet of the car, and peels the banana.

She looks me in the eye as she bites off the tip of the banana, then laughs. She says nothing else as she chomps down on it, filling her mouth every time, then discards the banana skin inches from my face.

"I love Shakespeare," she announces. "Do you like Shakespeare?"

I try to frown. My face doesn't move.

"Of course you don't – silly me! Unless it's got a pair of tits and a weak-willed woman, you don't give a shit, do you?"

Her legs swing side to side. She has something in her pocket. Something she collected from the house.

Oh, shit, it's my hunter's knife.

"My favourite play is Macbeth. Now, those who are super-stitious say you should not call it Macbeth as it's bad luck, especially in the theatre – they say you should call it *The Scottish Play*. But that's for people who believe in luck, isn't it?"

She stands. Wanders back and forth, balancing the knife on her finger, then dangling it, then pricking a spot of blood from the tip of her finger with its blade.

"It's about betrayal, but it's also about vengeance. Lady Macbeth goes mad, Macbeth goes mad, everything goes wrong because they decided to mess with King Duncan – a man that everyone admired."

She stops. Goes to her knees in front of me. Strokes my face in a way that might seem loving but is purely psychotic.

"Now, it's not the story that I'm making parallels from, it's actually my favourite line from that play. It's at the beginning, when people are talking about how violent Macbeth was in battle, and one of them says, and I quote, 'he unseamed him from the nave to th'chops.' Quite graphic, huh?"

She takes the knife and places the tip of the blade against my belly button.

"I always wondered what that would actually look like. I mean, it's pretty gross. You'd have to start from the nave."

She pokes the knife harder into my belly button.

"Then finish at the chops."

She puts a finger by my mouth.

"But see, I don't need to do it to you to know what it looks like. You've already shown me on an innocent little cat."

She leans toward me and whispers, "But I bet that's not the only time you've wrecked a pussy, is it?"

She places both hands on the knife and pushes it into my belly, digging it further and further, pressing harder and harder, until she's penetrated my muscle, and she draws blood.

"Now let's see what it's like to wreck this little pussy, shall we?"

No more warning. No hesitation. She stands and uses all of her body weight to plunge the knife further into my belly, and I scream and moan and it comes out as guttural utterances and blood that dribbles down my nose and my eyes.

She places both hands on the knife and, without taking it from my body, drags it downwards with all of the strength she can muster, dragging it and dragging it, taking it down my pectorals, only to find that my rib cage is too tough to penetrate. She has to take the knife out and stick it into the gaping wound of my belly, stick it further and further in, then twists it further in, and my intestine stumbles out and she punctures a lung and it fills with blood and I can't breathe, I can't breathe, I can't fucking breathe.

She finishes the last of my unseaming by returning my knife to the end of the wound at the base of my throat and dragging it across my neck and to my jaw.

Blood pours down my open face and my insides move around and I can see nothing – the blood is over my eyes – but I can feel wriggling around my body, like things are moving and shifting where they shouldn't, and I am trying desperately to breathe but I can't and it's almost over and she's laughing I think she's laughing I think I can hear laughing and the pain is too much and then suddenly–

Suddenly, nothing.

The misery ends, and I am done.

Fuck.

KACEY'S STORY

CHAPTER THIRTY-THREE

SOMETIMES I FIND myself walking past the police station, though I'm not sure why.

I imagine walking in, but I don't know what I'd say.

We killed a man.

We raped him, and we raped his wife.

But I'm not sure if I feel guilty for what we did, or worried that she got away.

And that is why I don't go in.

I stand outside and watch as police officers enter and leave. Their uniform terrifies me. It's a symbol of the difference between freedom and incarceration, and it makes my knees quiver.

Maybe I should just go in and confess?

But what of Pitbull? I couldn't do that to him. Or Jonno, despite Pitbull insisting that we cut him out of our lives

"We don't need to be surrounded by that kind of stupidity. If the police show up, it will be his fault."

Or mine, if I told the truth.

Then again, the stakes aren't as high for me, are they? I wasn't the one who left their semen inside of her.

I wasn't the one who killed her husband.

God, her husband…

Pitbull feels nothing. He makes love to me and rides me and anyone else I bring home, just as he has always done. He eats his rack of ribs with his hands, and rips pulled pork apart with his teeth, and turns the steak in the frying pan with the dead skin of his fingers – and he feels nothing.

But those hands…

I love what they do to me. But what they did to her…

Sometimes at night, I lie awake, wondering if it was his first assault. We've been married for eight years, together for ten. When I met him he had a reputation. He was a football hooligan. An alcoholic. A brutal thug. But I've seen none of that. My husband may not take any shit, but I've only ever seen him act calmly.

But there are moments…

When he reads, he only reads books by ex-gangsters. When we watch crime documentaries about police procedure, he stays quiet, like he's studying it. And when someone has a complaint about the service done on their car…

Let's just say I never see someone complain more than once.

But he's older now. Quieter. He's not just Pitbull, he's Jacob. And he's my Jacob.

And I couldn't do this to him.

I couldn't have him locked up because of me.

That woman had it coming. She did. Walking around with her upper-middle-class strut, and those sexy little dresses, and that pretty, vulnerable face. What did she think was going to happen?

Women like that are asking to be used.

I turn away from the police station. Continue across town. Past the tattooist who did my sleeve and my nose piercing. Past the bookies where Pitbull wastes his money. Past the statue of some guy I don't know and don't care to find out about.

Until I reach my solicitor's office. And I climb up the stairs – two floors of them – and enter.

"Hello?"

"Kacey Evans, here to–"

"Yes, they are waiting for you. You're late."

I check my watch. I am late. Damn.

She leads me through to a board room. Inside is a long table. On one side is Clifford, my lawyer. On the other side is Duncan, my ex, and his lawyer, whatever his name is.

"Mrs Evans, nice of you to join us," his lawyer says, a smug smirk wiped across his face. He looks like Nigel Farage and I want to slap him.

Clifford waves me over with a resolved glance – one that tells me we've already lost – and I sit beside him.

Duncan glares at me. I don't look at him.

"Wonderful," his lawyer says. "Now you've been kind enough to grace us with your presence, we shall begin."

I hate this sarcastic prick and I wish Pitbull was here – he would never let a man talk to me like that.

The lawyer shuffles through a few papers before settling on the one he's after.

"Right, so what is it you want?" the lawyer asks me.Clifford answers on my behalf.

"Joint custody."

"Joint?" The lawyer looks at Duncan and they exchange a smug grin.

"Yes, joint."

"Not visitation rights? Not even allowance to see the children, alone, in a halfway house? But joint custody?"

"That is what we would like."

The lawyer can't help but laugh. "I will remind you that the judge ruled against that."

"We plan to appeal."

"On what grounds?"

"On it being ethically wrong. Tracey and Colin deserve to have both her parents in her life."

Duncan laughs. I shoot him a look. He enjoys it.

"Okay, well then I shall ask you, Kacey," the lawyer says, turning to me. "The judge ruled against you having parental rights because you are living with, and are married to, a man with quite an extensive criminal record. Two counts of GBH, sexual assault of a teenager, theft, domestic abuse, drunk and disorderly – I mean, shall I go on?"

I shake my head.

"So are you still living with this man?" he asks.

"All of that was in his twenties," I say. "He's forty-two now, give him a break."

"Right, well I shall ask you again, are you still living with Jacob Evans? Or Pitbull, as I believe he is often referred to?"

Duncan laughs. "Fuck off," I snap at him, and I feel Clifford's hand on my arm.

"The question, please, Ms Evans," Duncan's lawyer prompts me.

"Yes, all right, I am still living with him. He's my husband, isn't he?"

The lawyer leans back and opens his arms. "Then I don't see what case you have. The judge ruled against your involvement in Tracey and Colin's life so long as your husband is in the picture. And you think he will change his mind?"

"I think you've made your point," Clifford interjects, and I feel grateful.

"Yes, but come on, what are we even doing here?" Duncan's lawyer persists. "You have no case."

"We are appealing the judge's ruling," Clifford says. "You will find that Mr Evans' criminal record has been clean for over a decade now. There is no reason to believe he is a present threat."

"Is his record clean, or has he just not been caught?"

"As far as you're concerned, it is clean. Now, we really do not wish to drag this through the courts again, and we wish to settle it here. Can we do that? Can we find a compromise?"

Duncan and his lawyer exchange a look, whereby Duncan gives the slightest of headshakes.

"I'm sorry, but no," the lawyer says. "The safety of the children is Duncan's priority, and–"

"No it isn't," I say, and I know I shouldn't, but I can't help it. "They are just weapons to use against me. Besides, aren't they teenagers now? Shouldn't they be able to make up their own mind?"

"The eldest is twelve, and no, they are still protected by the law – thank God. Now, unless there is a legitimate case you wish to make, I think we are done here, no?"

He looks at me, at Clifford, then at Duncan.

"Right, then."

He stands and leaves. Duncan follows him out, and he can't help but fire a wink my way, and Clifford's hand on my shoulder stops me from charging after him.

Once they are gone, I turn to Clifford and say, "Well? Are we going to appeal?"

Clifford shrugs. "We can, but I really don't see what the point is."

"What?"

"We won't win. And if we have to bring the kids in as witnesses, it's just more trauma for them."

"So you're saying I should just forget about seeing my kids?"

"No. There is one way you can see them."

"What? What way?"

Clifford sighs. Leans forward.

"Jacob," he says, and I stand and I throw my arms into the air. This man is meant to be my lawyer, and he's about as useful as a dick on a priest.

"Really? That's it?"

"He's a violent man, Kacey."

"No, he *was* violent. His record has been clean for ages, he's not–"

"Everyone else can see what he's capable of, Kacey. Why can't you?"

"You can't give up this case on what you think a man could or couldn't do. You should base it on the facts – he has not been convicted of anything in at least the past fifteen years."

"But he is clearly capable."

"Oh, fuck this."

I charge to the door. Turn back. "I pay you to be on my side, you know."

"You pay me to be honest, Kacey. An appeal would be a waste of your money. We can do it, but–"

"Then do it."

"Kacey…"

"I said do it. Send me the bill. My husband is happy to pay the costs. He's nice like that, you see."

Clifford sighs, gives a resolved shrug, and says, "Fine."

I leave. Not looking at the secretary. Not looking at anyone. Walking through town with my hood up and my hands in my pockets, glaring in the direction of anyone who dares look toward me.

I reach my car, still fuming, and drive home.

But when I get home, I will not tell Pitbull about this.

I will tell him we are going to appeal, but not about Duncan's demands.

Because I'm not sure what Pitbull will do if I tell him. And killing my children's father won't help to bring them back to me.

CHAPTER THIRTY-FOUR

I RETURN to the shop and there is an Audi in need of an MOT and a Volkswagen needing two tyres changed, as well as a note by the till from Pitbull saying he's gone out for the afternoon, and he needs me to mind the shop. He's lost his phone, and this is how he communicates with me now.

He's been disappearing like this a lot recently, and I know why.

He's searching.

For *her.*

He's getting in touch with various impounds and second-hand car dealerships to see if the jeep has come in. He's found her home address and is watching it day after day, as if she's going to return to it. He's phoning hospitals and pretending to be a relative looking for their darling Lisa.

So far, he has found nothing, and it makes him live in fear.

He had a brief stint in prison in his late teens, and he said he'd die before he went back. And although he thinks he hides it, I feel him next to me at night, lying awake. I see him googling her name every now and then. I see him sitting pensively, wondering, plotting, scheming – trying to come up with another lead that will help him find her.

Jonno has stopped calling the store, which is good. He was doing it every few days, begging for forgiveness, but we haven't heard from him for the past week or so. Pitbull was pretty adamant about cutting Jonno out of our lives, and I didn't want to go against him. Maybe now the guy's taken the hint.

I get to work, trying not to think about where Pitbull might be. Which county, at which hospital, or at which house. He spent most of last night on her Facebook account, which had been inactive for a while, but had allowed him to find the names of her parents and siblings and cousins. Perhaps he's going to each of their houses, looking for her.

I would wonder what he's going to do when he finds her, but there is no doubt in my mind what he will do.

And I try not to think about it.

Try not to think about *her*.

Or what Pitbull is planning.

I jack up the Volkswagen, detach the wheel and remove it. Then I use the mounting machine so the bead breaker can detach the tyre wall from the rim. It keeps my mind occupied. I've always been good at fixing things. It's what I like to do. It keeps me busy. Even so, I continue my work on automatic, and my mind wanders again.

I wish Pitbull would find his phone. Or get a new one. Just so I can ring him and find out where he is and if he's okay. I'm worried about him. He's not sleeping and he's not resting. He'll burn out if he keeps going like this.

Maybe it would be easier for him if the police just showed up at our door. At least then, he'd know.

But then again, he'd end up in prison for the rest of his life, so maybe not.

I finish up the Volkswagen and begin the MOT on the Audi. I check the lights are correctly positioned and show the correct colour, check the horn, check the battery, the electrical wiring, then move onto the steering wheel.

Within half an hour, the MOT is done, and I can't find anything to fail it on. Normally we find something so we can earn a bit of extra money by having to fix it, but today I can't be arsed – I want to go home early and have a bath, and that means finishing work without having to pretend to fix something.

I ring the cars' owner and they return and pick them up. It reaches five and the shop is dead, so I shut up and return to my car. I stink of gas and oil. My white vest is stained, and my jeans are grubby.

And I miss my husband.

Where is he?

I stop off at the supermarket to pick up some bubble bath, and some white wine that I'll no doubt finish off alone, and return to the car.

When I do, I find a text message alert on my phone. It's from Pitbull.

He must have found his phone!

```
Hey babe, hurry home. Don't bother with
a bath or shower — I like you grubby.
Just come to the bedroom straight away.
I have a surprise for you…
```

I can't help smiling. I even pump my fist. I can't wait. Maybe he's found her, and he's dealt with her – or maybe he's given up. Either way, I don't care. I'm just glad that he's wanting to spend time with me now, and a bit of kinkiness with my husband is exactly what I need.

And a surprise too... I wonder what it could be...

I speed home, accelerating through every green light and ignoring every irritated horn.

When I arrive, I rush out of my car and into the house, unable to contain my excitement.

CHAPTER THIRTY-FIVE

THE DOOR UNLOCKS and the house is dark and still. Like there's nobody home.

At first, I'm confused. He told me to rush home.

Then I turn on the hallway light and I see it.

An envelope is attached to the bannister. Roses across the floor and up the stairs. The faint tune of a piano coming from the stereo upstairs.

I can't help but smile. I'm like any woman – I need to be fucked, but I also need to be romanced. And when the two entwine, that's when I really get goosepimples.

I take the envelope. Open it. Inside is a folded piece of parchment. I open that and read, in printed italics:

I'M SORRY I'VE BEEN SUCH A GRUMP RECENTLY.
THINGS HAVEN'T BEEN EASY, BUT I DON'T WANT YOU TO
FORGET HOW MUCH YOU MATTER.
SO COME UPSTAIRS, NICE AND SLOWLY. I'M WAITING.

I hold it to my chest. Beam so much my light could overwhelm the sun.

It's like when we first started dating. He'd leave flowers for when I arrived home all the time. He'd write me notes. He'd play music.

Don't mistake me, I love what we have now. I get turned on by how he gets turned on when I fuck other men. I love watching them fuck him too. And I love fucking each other at the end of it all.

But I also loved what we had then.

I adore him, and I want to be adored. Especially recently, as he's felt so distant. And this is how he makes me feel wanted again.

I place the note in my pocket, wanting to save it. I pick up the first rose. Its petals are blood-red. I hold it beneath my nose and enjoy its scent.

I follow the rest of the roses upstairs. They lead me closer to bliss, and with every step my heart beats faster.

But I take it slowly. Just as he said.

He likes it when I do what he says.

When I reach the top of the steps, the roses turn into rose petals, leading me toward the closed bedroom door.

There is another envelope taped to it.

I giggle like a schoolgirl. It's silly but I don't care. I feel special. Important. Desired. Everything we pretend we don't need, but we do, oh we do – everyone wants to be desired, and everyone wants a partner to show them that they are desired.

I take the envelope. Open it. Again, in printed italics, it reads:

I'M WAITING IN THE OTHER ROOM. I WILL COME IN ONCE YOU'RE READY.

I look over my shoulder. The door to the spare room is closed. Just the thought that he's in there, waiting, is enough to turn me on.

I open the door. Gentle piano music creates the ambience. The petals continue across the floor and onto the bed.

On each corner of the bed are restraints. Leather ankle cuffs at the end. Handcuffs at the headboard. Another envelope on the duvet, next to a blindfold.

He'll have the keys and I'll be helpless and he will be in complete control and *shit* it gets me going…

Like I said – a woman needs to be fucked and romanced. I've been romanced – and now I'm ready to be fucked.

I take the final envelope and open it.

I THINK YOU KNOW WHAT I WANT YOU TO DO.

Oh, yes, yes I do, Pitbull, yes I do, Jacob, yes I do, my love!

I take off my vest. Take off my jeans. Ignore the smell of a day's work because I know he likes it. He says my body odour may stink to everyone else – but to him it's heavenly. It's my scent. And it's so animalistic of him, and I love it, and I take off my bra and my panties until I am naked and helpless.

But not helpless enough. Not yet.

I climb onto the bed, kneeling on the petals, taking a handful and crushing them in my fist. I place an ankle through the first restraint and tighten it – hard – tight enough that I will feel a little tinge of pain every time I move – and I do the same with the other ankle.

Then I pick up the blindfold. I smell it. It's new. It's not the one we normally use.

Oh, I can't wait to find out what he has planned, what he's going to do to me. I hope he starts slow then gets fast… Chokes me as I cum… Tells me I'm a dirty little bitch but that I'm *his* dirty little bitch while I am just too helpless to disagree…

I put the blindfold on. Tighten it, then double knot it and

tighten it again. It won't come off, not even with a shitload of friction.

I reach my right arm back and find the handcuff, place my wrist in, and close it with a satisfying click.

I couldn't get out of this if I wanted to. Not now. Not ever.

He has the key.

He is in charge now.

And I can't fucking wait!

I place my left arm through the next handcuff and bend my hand enough to tighten it around my wrist. They are a little hard on arms, and the pain is already adding to the very much anticipated pleasure.

I turn my head toward where I know the open door is – I can't see a bloody thing in this blindfold! – and I call out to him.

"Honey, I'm here and I'm helpless, I hope you're not going to hurt me!"

I giggle and it's silly but it's all just part of the act.

There is a pause, a moment where I think he's not there, then I hear the bedroom door down the end of the hallway creak open, ever so slightly, and the lightest of footsteps emerge.

He's taking it slowly. Teasing me. Tantalising me. *Tormenting* me.

The footsteps, one by one, walk faintly across the carpet, then pause, probably in the doorway, probably to look at me.

To admire.

His beautiful, naked wife, bound and restrained, wet and helpless.

I smile. Giggle again. He knows he's taunting me and I know he's taunting me and the anticipation of it already has me aroused enough – I think he's not going to need to fuck me for long until I give him the first screaming orgasm he desires.

"Enjoy what you see?" I ask.

He doesn't reply.

He remains silent. In control. His footsteps move slowly around the bed. I can picture him, removing his top as he goes, revealing his muscular torso, then removing his trousers and his boxers until he stands naked over his helpless wife, still turned on by her after all these years.

He stands there, and he says nothing. And he stands there. And he says nothing. And I am starting to get cold.

"Come on…" I say. "I need to be punished…"

Still, he doesn't move. I can hear him breathing, deep and heavy, but his thick biceps don't press down the mattress and his heaving breath doesn't pant over my face.

"Come on, it's not like you've not seen this before…"

Finally, the mattress sinks and I assume it's his knee, then it sinks again and I assume it's his other knee.

"Finally… I was starting to think you were going to let me get away with being so naughty…"

His arms land either side of my waist and he crawls, over my body, and I am breathing hard and fast and just waiting, waiting for him to touch me, to rub me, to lick me, to *fuck* me…

The tip of a finger lands on my neck and he runs it down between my breasts and over my nipple and down my navel and stops by my inner thigh – right where I want him to keep going – and I moan in frustration and arousal.

"Oh, come on, keep going!"

But he doesn't.

He just stays there, over me, breathing on me, not touching me.

"Come on you big brute… What, you want me to work you up first?"

He does. I can tell.

He loves it when I verbally abuse him.

It just makes him want to hurt me more.

"You fat prick… You vile bastard… You ugly piece of shit…"

His face comes closer to mine, I can feel his breath getting warmer, and his lips hover over my lips, almost touching, and then he speaks, he finally speaks:

"Ugly? I thought you said I was pretty."

What?

That's not his voice.

That's not even a man's voice.

That's…

I start screaming and kicking, but no matter how much I pull on the handcuffs and the restraints it does not change how helpless I am.

And now I know how she felt.

CHAPTER THIRTY-SIX

"Please... Please..."

"Please?"

She mocks me with her tone. I don't blame her. She begged. Did I listen?

"But you're going to have such a good time..." she says.

I did this.

I said those words, and I created this monster, and this is all my fault, and it is what I deserve.

"Please, I know what we did was wrong..."

She laughs, but says nothing else. I can still feel her breath on my face and her body over mine. She remains there, probably enjoying it, and I don't blame her.

I truly don't blame her.

"What we did was wrong, I really mean that."

Even as I say the words, I realise how little impact they will have. They are fickle. Trying to appeal to her conscience or trying to assure her that I have changed or trying to make her see that I know we shouldn't have done what we did – it's futile. Pointless.

Yet I try anyway.

"It was Pitbull and Jonno who did it... You should do this to them, not me... I was just the facilitator, they were the ones who hurt you."

She chuckles.

And I wonder.

We haven't heard from Jonno in a while. Despite blanking him, we'd still get drunken calls or desperate text messages, and we've had nothing in a long time.

And my husband...

How does she have my husband's phone?

"What have you done to him?"

She laughs again. The bed moves as she gets up. I don't know where she is now.

"What have you done to my husband?"

She doesn't reply.

"Please don't hurt him..."

"I thought he was the one who hurt me, though. Not you. Isn't that right?"

"Yes. No. I..."

I wish I could see her. If I could beseech her with my eyes, if I could look her in the face, maybe, just maybe, she could see how sorry I am.

But it's not enough. In this situation, an apology almost seems to be an insult.

"Please, take this blindfold off."

Nothing.

"Please, at least let me look at you."

Still nothing.

"Please..."

Movement. She's at my side. She reaches behind me and undoes the knot – both of them – she struggles as I tie good knots – and she lets the blindfold off and I look at her.

She's thinner than she was. I mean, she was thin before, but now she looks unhealthy. There are bags under her eyes.

Her hair is greasy. She looks like she's been living under a bridge.

I go to ask her if she is okay, but stop myself. What a stupid question.

"I haven't hurt your husband yet, you don't need to worry," she tells me.

There is only one word in that sentence I can focus on, and I repeat it back to her: "*Yet?*"

"But you might want to see this."

She takes out an iPhone. It's Pitbull's iPhone. How did she get it?

She unlocks it and shows me a picture.

It's Jonno. Upside down. His chest split open and his face crusted with blood. He's almost unrecognisable; if it weren't for tracksuit bottoms and the shaved head, I'd almost think it was an imposter.

But that is Jonno. And that's his garage. And that's Pitbull's old rope pulley.

Did she do that to him?

Damn…

"You're going to kill me, aren't you?"

She smiles like you'd smile to a stupid child asking stupid questions.

"Look, we'll go to the police. I almost went to the police a few times, but I'm ready now, really – you can untie me, and we'll go together, and we'll tell them everything that Jonno and Pitbull did."

"That Jonno and Pitbull did?"

I gulp. "That *we* did."

"What if I don't want to go to the police? What if I'm already doing exactly what I want to do?"

"You aren't. I know your type. You care for animals, you give to charity, you probably work as a teacher or a nurse or something – you aren't the murderous type. You're the compassionate type, and I know you won't hurt me. I know you won't. You're too nice."

She walks over to me. Kneels down. At first, I think she's going to untie me. But she doesn't. She reaches under the bed. Stares at me as she does it. Fiddles around, and brings out a knife.

Pitbull's hunter's knife. The one he killed her husband with.

She stares at my bare chest. At my navel. Like she's undressing my skin. Like she's deciding on the best target.

"You won't," I assure her. "You won't.

She holds the knife with both hands and raises it high above her head.

"Your husband wouldn't want you to do this."

She pauses. Looks at me. I feel hope. Amongst the dreaded fear, I feel a tinge of promise that I found what will appeal to her morality.

"Michael, that was his name, wasn't it?"

She frowns. I can't tell if she's angry or reluctant.

"Michael was a kind man too. If he was here, he'd want you to go to the police. He'd want you to do this the proper way – to have a fair trial, which I will plead guilty at and testify against my husband if I must – and he will want you to avoid having any more blood on your hands."

She tilts her head. She's examining me. But I see potential. I see empathy. I see kindness.

"You are a good person, and good people don't deserve to have things like this weighing on their conscience."

I think she's backing off. I think it's worked. I breathe a sigh of relief, grateful that I may still get to keep my life after all.

"I know you won't do it," I tell her. "You're a good person, and you won't."

And then she does.

With all the strength her bony body can muster, she thrusts the knife downwards, landing it in my belly, and it feels uncomfortable, at first. Like someone's put something where it shouldn't go. Then she pushes it harder, and the blood trickles over my waist and onto the sheets, and the pain is excruciating, and I try to breathe, only to find that I can't, and the pain intensifies further and I try to breathe again, but I can't, and I try again and I can't and I stare at the wall as I realise – I am about to die.

She takes the knife out and its agony and I wheeze without air.

I try calling her a bitch but I can't form the letters.

Then, with this crazed look in her eyes, like a wild beast tormenting its supper, she lifts the knife and swings it with all her might into the side of my neck, and it feels like my breath is trapped, somewhere inside my body, and I can't get it, and my heart slows and the world grows fuzzy and she just stands there.

Still.

Unmoved.

Watching me.

Relishing the moment.

And I can't say a word and I can't object and I can't do a thing to stop what's happening.

I don't want to die.

I really don't.

I want a future with Pitbull. I want to get my kids back. Maybe have another one. Expand the business. Get back in touch with my mum.

There's so much I want to do.

And I desperately want to do it.

But I won't.

I can't.

Something fills my mouth and my nostrils and I'm fairly certain it's blood.

The last thing I see is her eyes. There's red in them, I'm sure.

Then my head flops to the side.

And I become still.

And I don't think anymore.

PITBULL'S STORY

CHAPTER THIRTY-SEVEN

FOR THE FIFTH day in a row, I drive up the motorway and take the junction nearest to her hometown. I cruise through the streets until I reach her estate, and I drive by her house to find the garden still overgrown and the same parcel on her porch that was there weeks ago.

I go past her workplace and wait outside. People leave, but none of them are her.

Then I go to her parent's house, and this is where I stay. Down the road, always parking in the same place so someone thinks I'm a resident.

Finding out this information wasn't hard. On her Facebook profile, there is a picture of her and Michael outside their new house, the number 52 behind them. Also on her profile is a photograph of the street, which is easy enough to put into Google images and find a street that matches. She also has her occupation in the *about* section of her Facebook profile, which I use to find her place of work, and there is a video of her outside her parents' home from a few years ago that I use to find out her parents' address.

I linger outside her parents' house because they seem to be

the ones who care most about her absence. I've seen them leave every now and then wearing *Find Lisa* t-shirts. Their family liaison officer occasionally drops in. I can often see them through the window, crying into their cheese board or prawn sandwiches or whatever the fuck it is rich pricks eat.

But, as yet, there has been no clue as to where she is.

I don't understand it.

Why didn't she go straight to the police?

Unless she's dead. She may have crashed the jeep in her crazed state. But if that's the case, then why hasn't her body been identified, and why can't I track down my jeep?

I rest my elbow on the window and my chin on my fist. My knee is shaking up and down. I feel anxious and I don't know how to stop it.

I just hate knowing she's out there.

I know Kacey thinks I'm obsessed, but it's not her who'll be sent to prison, is it? They'd would have found mine and Jonno's semen in the bitch, not hers – not that I give a shit if Jonno goes to prison, as that imbecile created this mess by letting her escape.

I'd kill him if I thought he mattered enough to kill. As it is, I'm sure he'll be miserable enough being on his own. Not even his mum cares enough to visit him.

I put the radio on and keep watching the house. A bunch of blokes are arguing about whether or not Arsenal could surprise the league this season. I snort. The only people Arsenal will surprise is their fans when they realise how shit they are.

I huff. This is tedious, but it needs to be done. If I'm ever going to sleep at night, I need to find out what's happened to her.

If she's dead, I need to know there's a corpse.

If she's missing, I need to know why.

If she's alive, I need to kill her.

Half an hour passes. The idiots on the radio leave Arsenal alone as the news starts. Some politician is being a dickhead again. What a surprise.

Then I spot them in my rear-view mirror. The filth, approaching in their yellow, blue and white car. They don't even try to be inconspicuous, do they?

The car pulls up out outside the house. Two police officers get out. They tuck their hands beneath their stab-proof vests and walk with the same arrogance they all walk with. One is a man, maybe late twenties, and the other is a woman, a little older but way too small to be a copper. I'd like to see her try and face off with me when I'm wasted and pissed off.

They approach the house, but they don't remove their hats. It's not bad news. But it might be news.

They haven't noticed me, but I check my weapons just in case.

Next to my ankle is my knife, the blade curved and sharp, ready to slice apart anyone who tries to manhandle me into the back of a car.

I open the glove compartment. My two grenades remain inside. They cost me a fair bit, but it was worth it. The moment the roz even thinks about coming for me, I will remove the pin and send pieces of their body flying in every direction. The surrounding houses will look like a police pizza once those have gone off.

I shut the glove compartment. Watch the house. The piggies stay in there for about ten minutes, then walk out, return to their car, and drive away.

The girl's mother remains on the porch. Another woman stands next to her with arms around her, possibly a sister or friend. They are talking and I want to know what they are saying so I wind down my window, turn the ignition, and drive down the street as slowly as I can.

"I'm sure she'll show up," I hear the woman say.

It seems there is still no news.

I drive on, leave the estate, and direct myself to the motorway.

I could go home. I know Kacey would want that. But she needs to understand the stakes of this situation – I can't go home when she wants me to be home. I can't be the doting husband, not while this risk remains out there, free to think she's beaten me.

I can't rest until I've killed this cunt.

CHAPTER THIRTY-EIGHT

ON THE WAY HOME, I stop off at a shop to buy a cheap phone. I can't seem to find mine. Then I find an internet café that's open late and pay for an hour on a computer.

I always use an internet café, and I always use a fake name, and I never use the same one twice. I don't want any smart-arse lawyers trying to use my internet history against me – how would it look if I was arrested and the police could see that I was looking for this bitch this whole time?

I search for hospitals on Google Maps. I've already tried all the ones within a thirty miles radius from home, so I extend it to forty miles. It gives me another three.

I phone the closest one first. Some impatient woman answers. I hate hospital receptionists – they are so fed up of dealing with arseholes they fail to realise they've become one too.

I tell her I'm looking for my sister who went missing months ago, and wanted to check they don't have any Jane Does that haven't been identified. They don't. They have two coma patients, and they are both male. They look back through the history and find that they haven't had anyone matching the description in the past three months.

I phone the other two with similar stories. Only, instead of saying sister I say daughter, and then wife. Similar answers. Nothing.

I sit back and kick the table leg in frustration, even though I knew that I'd find nothing, because that's all I find – nothing.

I search obituaries. Funeral services. Death announcements. I find public records on death certificates.

I've already searched these exact things, over and over, but I search them again – finding the exact same results.

I move onto the jeep. It's due its MOT, and I know it's ridiculous to think this woman would have taken it in for an MOT, but I search the MOT records for the jeep anyway. It has a perfect record of passing MOTs – of course it will, I did all of them. But there is no record of it having had its MOT, and this website makes it clear that it's overdue.

I lean back. Run my hands over my face. I consider texting Kacey. I could do with hearing her voice right now.

Not that I'd admit that to her. Or anyone.

Pitbull is a tough sonofabitch, and he doesn't need anyone to make him feel better.

But I really wish I could hear Kacey's voice, just for a minute.

I dial Kacey's phone number, put it to my ear, and listen.

It just rings.

Over and over.

No answer at all.

"Hi, this is Kacey, I can't get to the phone at the moment so please leave a message and I just might think about calling you back."

I hear the beep.

"Hey, babe. It's me. I still can't find my phone, so I got some cheap new one so I could call you. Listen, er… give me a ring back, yeah? See you later."

I hang up. Stare at the phone screen.

It's strange that she doesn't answer.

Kacey lives on her phone. In work, she'll have her headphones in. On the way home, she'll be listening to a podcast on it. When she arrives home, she'll be on Facebook and iMessage and all those shitty apps I couldn't care less about, but she seems to spend all evening on.

And she always answers her phone, even to an unknown number.

Perhaps she's on the toilet.

Then again, she always takes her phone into the bathroom with her. She can't take a piss without playing another game of Candy Crush.

Screw it. I'll ring again later.

I need a drink.

I return to my car and put an audiobook on. Reggie Kray's biography. It's the third time I'm listening to it and it's still teaching me new things.

I put my local pub into my SatNav. I have a two-hour drive. I'm tired, thirsty, and in desperate need of a beer.

I set off, shooting down the motorway at ninety, glancing at my new phone every few minutes.

Kacey does not call back.

CHAPTER THIRTY-NINE

I GO by the shop on the way, wondering if Kacey is working late. It's shut. No sign of life at all. I grumble under my breath and carry on to the pub.

I enter and Carl – the barman – nods at me.

"The usual?" he asks.

I give him a slight nod then lean on the bar and look around. The normal crowd is in. A few guys I went to school with play pool in the corner. A few guys I know by sight play darts. The retirees sit in silence at their table, nothing to say and nothing to live for.

Some young squirt puts some money in the jukebox and scrolls through the options.

"Oi!" I aim at him.

He looks around.

"You."

He looks at me timidly. Why do kids in their early twenties always look like they are about to be hit by a car when you talk to them? Like they are scared of everything.

"Me?" he asks.

"Yeah. You better select something good. I'm listening to no shit."

He nods. Takes a deep breath. Clearly changes his mind about whatever crap he was about to choose. He selects something, then turns to me expectantly.

Sweet Child of Mine by Guns & Roses starts playing.

I nod. "Well done, kid. Solid choice."

I turn back to the bar as Carl puts a pint of Stella in front of me.

"On your tab, Pitbull?"

"Yes, mate."

I take the pint, drink a few gulps, and walk over to a table in the far corner. I sit on the edge of a stool and watch the regulars live out their monotonous lives. I don't notice that I'm tearing up the beer mat with my spare hand.

I check the phone. Still nothing.

I stop feeling peeved and start feeling angry. What the fuck is that woman playing at? She better be dead or incapacitated if she's not replying to me. I don't like to be made a fool of.

I take another few mouthfuls of beer. Some scrawny fucker walks out of the toilets and stumbles to the bar. I recognise him. He's a bloke Kacey brought home a few months ago. He lasted two minutes inside of her before he blew his load. One of the most pathetic dickheads we've ever allowed into our bedroom.

Another few gulps and I've almost finished the beer.

The scrawny guy turns to me. His face flickers with recognition. I glare at him, but he doesn't take the hint. He just keeps staring, trying to figure out where he knows me from.

"Hey," he says, and falls over a stool as he stumbles toward me. "Don't I know you?"

Does this idiot have a death wish or what?

He uses the bar to balance himself and walk toward me, too drunk to know what he's doing is stupid.

"No, yeah, I do, where do I know you…"

"How about you back the fuck off, yeah?"

"No, wait, I know you, I do…"

I huff. Grip my beer glass.

"Hey, how about you mind your own business?" Carl tries to tell this guy, but he just doesn't take the hint.

"It's okay," he says, slurring his words. "He's a mate, I know he is, I–"

He points to the ceiling as realisation hits him.

"I know where I know you from!"

I grip my beer glass even harder. If he says it, I'm going to break his face.

"Yeah, that's right…"

Carl glances over. He knows what's coming. Most of the pub has fallen silent, knowing what's imminent.

"I remember!" The man leans over me. "Didn't I fuck your wife?"

I throw the last drop of beer over his head then smash the glass against his face. It separates into many large shards and a few of them remain in his cheek, poking out of his skin.

He stumbles back and I stand over him. Grab his hair. Lift him up, then strike his head against the bar.

A few teeth clatter against the flooring.

I lift his head up again and ram it against the bar once more, leaving an imprint of blood from his nose.

I drop the guy and he stays on the floor, his eyes opening and closing, groaning as he rolls over.

I look around the pub. Every pair of eyes is on me. Absolute silence. A pause in the game of pool and a pause in the game of darts.

"Did you see anything?" I ask the room.

Silence responds.

I turn to Carl, and he says, "No one saw nothing, Pitbull. The guy was drunk. End of."

I look down at the prick. His eyes widen as he stares up at me. The fear in his eyes gives me a rush. There's no better high than making a grown man piss his pants.

"Good," I tell Carl, then look around the room. People lower their faces and divert their gaze away.

I step over the bloody-faced coward and stomp out of the pub, returning to my car, and wait for my anger to subside.

As much as it can do, anyway. The rage is never gone. Not completely. It's always there, inside of me, waiting to come out.

And that is why no one in their right mind would fuck with me. Not some twat in his twenties. Not a roomful of drinkers. And especially not some stupid upper-middle-class bitch who thinks she can get away from me.

As my fury returns to its normal state, I decide it's not time to go home yet. Not whilst she's out there.

Not whilst she thinks she's won.

CHAPTER FORTY

I SIT behind the steering wheel, barely listening to the narrator of my audiobook nattering incessantly in the background. I practically know Kray's autobiography by heart anyway.

I try Kacey's phone again, holding it to my ear, letting it ring and ring and ring and ring.

"Hi, this is Kacey, I can't get to the phone at the moment so please leave a message and I just might think about calling you back."

"Kacey, what the fuck is going on? Why aren't you picking up my calls? I'm getting proper irritated. Get back to me. I'm going to head home soon, just going to do a run by the scrap yard first."

I hang up. Stare at the phone.

I'm a mixture of pissed off and concerned.

I swear, if I go home and she's sat there watching television without a care in the world, I am going to kick off.

I plan to do another check that my mate Tony's scrap yard hasn't had a jeep come in yet. It's closed, but I don't care. Tony will open it up for me if I tell him to.

That's what fear does, you see. It gives people a lot more impetus to help than politeness does.

I search for Tony's business card in the glove compartment. I move the grenades aside and find it. Dial it. Wait for him to answer.

"Hello?" he says.

"Tony, this is Pitbull."

"Pitbull? Hang on."

He sounds tired. Was probably in bed, and wants to move to another room so he doesn't wake his wife. After a bit of shuffling, he talks.

"You getting back to my message?"

"What message?"

"I left you an answer phone message."

"I lost my phone, Tony. What did it say?"

"That jeep you're looking for – we had one come in."

My heart beats a little faster.

"Is it mine?"

"I lost the license plate you wrote down, but it's the right model."

My leg shakes. My body comes to life. I sweat with anticipation.

"I'll meet you down the scrap yard," I tell him.

"Come on, man, it's midnight."

"And?"

I wait for him to come up with an excuse. A good reason for standing up to me. I don't expect one.

"Fine," he says. "Let me get dressed and I'll meet you down there."

He hangs up and I hang up and that's the *fear* I was talking about – and the impetus it produces.

I drive through various villages, staying under the speed limit – I don't want some overkeen young officer to think it's worth starting shit with me, not now, not when I'm this close

– and I arrive at the scrap yard before Tony does. I park outside, kill my lights, and get out. I peer through the bars and try to see if I can see the jeep.

I can't. It's too dark. Or Tony was smart and kept it hidden from view.

Tony shows up a few minutes later and pulls up next to my car. He gets out. He's wearing a crumpled shirt and jeans stained with coffee. He must have been in a hurry, which is good – it means he knows how much this matters.

"Hi, mate," he says.

"Evening."

He takes his keys out and unlocks the chains around the bars. Once done, he removes them, and opens the gates.

"This way," he tells me, and he leads me past numerous cars with various parts stripped from them. He tells me to wait, goes inside the office, and seconds later a floodlight comes on. He comes out again and leads me around the corner.

And there it is.

The jeep.

My jeep.

With the correct license plate.

He sees the look on my face and asks, "What's the big deal with this jeep, anyway?"

"Don't you worry about that, Tony, you beauty!" I pinch his cheeks and rush toward the jeep.

Tony looks over his shoulder and sees a figure approaching.

"That'll be security," he tells me, though I really don't care. "Give me a minute."

He rushes around the corner to do whatever he needs to do, leaving me alone with my vehicle.

It's still intact. There are no scratches on the paintwork, no smashed windows, not even a dent on its body.

I open the car door and look inside. The leather seats are

in pristine condition, the air freshener still dangles from the rear-view mirror, and there is only a light line of dust on the dashboard.

Which leads me to ask – why on earth would this be taken to a scrapyard when it's in such good condition?

Tony reappears around the corner.

"We only have two minutes, mate, we're not supposed to be here."

I ignore him. "How'd you get the car?"

"Huh?" he says, looking behind himself, and it annoys me how distracted he is.

"How did you get the car, Tony?"

"The car? Oh yeah, it was the weirdest thing. I came in yesterday morning, and it had just been left outside the gates. The keys were in the ignition and all. Someone had abandoned it here."

I stare at him, my mind torn with confusion.

Someone left it here?

Well, that someone was obviously *her*…

But why would she just leave it here? And with the keys? What was she doing?

Did she know I was looking at scrapyards? That I was looking here?

Is this a taunt?

A message?

Oh, how I wish that dainty little whore would try and deliver a message to my face. She'll learn all about the different kinds of pain once I'm done.

"Cheers, Tony," I say, and I give him a nod and direct myself out of the scrapyard, leaving the jeep behind and returning to my car.

I don't understand.

Who else could have done this?

I sit in the driver's seat and rest my head on my hand. I

don't turn the ignition on. I don't even move. I just sit, and think, though I'm not sure what I even think.

I'm just too confused.

I hear Tony locking up behind me. He knocks on my window and asks if I'm all right. I wave him away and he pisses off back to his car and drives back home to his irritable wife.

Why would she just leave the car here?

If it is a gibe, or an attempt at mocking me, I swear, I will grind her body into meat and pound on her flesh.

I've never felt as fucking angry as I do now.

I don't think I could get any angrier.

I pick up my phone. Time to go home. Before I do, I try Kacey one more time.

The phone rings. And rings. And rings.

And then she answers.

"Hello?"

"Kacey?"

"Who is this?"

"Kacey, it's me, why aren't you answering your fucking phone?"

She laughs.

Is she kidding?

"Why are you laughing, Kacey? Are you trying to piss me off?"

She keeps laughing, then as her chuckles come to an end, and she says, "This isn't Kacey."

"What?"

"I said this isn't Kacey. I'm afraid your wife can't talk right now."

"What? Why not? Put her on the phone!"

"I could do that, but she won't say much."

"What do you mean, she won't say much?"

"Dead bodies are notoriously silent."

Dead bodies?

What?

"Who is this?" I ask, but I already know the answer.

"Come home, Jacob," she says, and hangs up.

She god damn hangs up on me.

She's lying. She hasn't killed Kacey. She couldn't. She's not capable.

She's just a prissy little entitled bitch. They are too prim and proper to hurt anybody. I doubt she's had to fight for anything in her entire life.

I turn the ignition. My fury grinds my body into action. I pound my foot against the gas and skid onto the main road.

Funny, I was just thinking about how I couldn't get any angrier.

I was wrong.

CHAPTER FORTY-ONE

I SKID my car to a halt on the drive I tarmacked myself, kick the door of my new car open, and charge to the front door.

I turn the handle and it's locked.

I growl, unaware that I'm doing so, and fumble for my keys. My arms are shaking and I struggle to keep the keys still, but my frenzied hands eventually turn the lock and I barge my front door open.

The house is dark. Not a single light on. Plenty of places to hide.

"Kacey!" I shout.

There's no response. I bounce from one wall to another and knock the shoe rack over on my way through the hallway and into the living room.

"Kacey?"

I go to turn the light on, but it doesn't come on. My first instinct is to think the bulb has blown, and my second instinct is not to be so naïve. It's either the fuse box or the circuit breaker. She's done this on purpose.

I move through the living room, ensuring my wife isn't in here, then return to the hallway and into the kitchen.

"Kacey?"

She's not at the dining table or at the kitchen counter or in the utility room. I open the garden doors, look back and forth, scanning the bench and the pond and the plants.

I slam the doors shut and move to the stairs, pounding up them, not intending to be subtle.

If she's here, I want her to know I'm coming. I want her to try whatever she's going to try, and I want her to find out what happens when she tries it.

I look in the spare room. Nothing.

In the bathroom. Nothing.

Then I see, across the hallway, the door to our bedroom is half open, and Kacey's hand is hanging off the bed. I know it's hers as I can see her wedding band on her ring finger.

Is she asleep?

"Kacey?"

I don't move. Not yet. I don't know why. Self-preservation, perhaps. Who cares.

"Kacey, talk to me."

But she's not talking to me, and her arm isn't flinching, and it's laying in a really odd way that surely can't be comfortable.

My breath quivers as I take a wary step forward, followed by another and another. I reach the door and place my hand on it and give it a gentle nudge. It creaks open.

The first thing I register is the blood.

Nothing else makes sense. Not yet. It will in a minute, I'm sure, but for now, all I can see is the blood, and it's on the bed sheets and on the headboard and some is on the walls and a lot is on her body.

Her body.

Her body.

Oh god, her body.

She's not moving and I dive to her side but I already know that no amount of CPR or chest compressions is going to bring back someone who's had their throat slit like this. The open wound goes across the width of her neck in one thick line, and it gapes at me, her trachea or oesophagus or whatever it is clearly exposed.

And there's a wound in her belly. It's deep and the blood still glistens in the light of the moon from the open curtains.

"Kacey..."

My hand is on the back of her head, stroking her hair, and I am looking in her eyes but they don't look back. They stare upwards.

Was that where they were looking when *she* did this?

No. The death wouldn't have been instant. Not one like this. She would have had to lie there, suffocating, unable to breathe, knowing she was about to die, whilst *she* looked at her.

I don't think of *her* anymore. Not yet. For now, all I think of is my wife, and I try to understand what's going on. I know it's bad, but it doesn't make sense.

So I say the words.

I say them in a whisper that barely passes my lips.

"She's dead."

And I feel tears in my eyes and I don't give a shit if they aren't manly, they come out and dampen my cheeks and moisten my stubble and I punch the headboard, causing a dent in the wood and dead skin on my knuckles.

I scream. I roar. I want to turn this bed upside down and smash the windows yet at the same time I just want to crawl into a little ball, in the corner, and close my eyes in hope that when I open them this will not be real.

"Kacey..."

She was my wife.

She *is* my wife.

The only woman who ever understands me and my decisions and my past and my plans and my fetishes and...

And she's…

"Dead."

The image becomes clearer now. I begin to understand what's happened. What *she* has done to her.

I finally realise.

The woman I love has been murdered. Brutally. Sadistically. She's been tortured and tormented and I do not care about anything but making this bitch pay.

I stand. My body has tensed. I can't look at her anymore.

The blood is still wet. This can't have happened long ago. *She'll* be close by.

I know she will.

I limp to the wardrobe. I don't know why I'm limping, but I suddenly ache in my leg. I open the wardrobe doors and kneel so I can get to the safe. I punch in the combination and the door opens. I reach in. Grab my sawn-off shotgun. Grab the shells. Close the safe. Load the gun.

Stand up and point it at the door.

See Kacey out of the corner of my eye.

Pause. Try not to look. Try not to think.

I can think about it later. I can think about it when it's done.

Not now.

Please, not now.

"I'm dead now, darling."

Please, Kacey, don't.

"You know what you have to do."

Stop talking. You're dead, so stop talking.

"Now stop being such a pussy and do it."

Yes.

Yes, Kacey.

I will.

I march to the door, shotgun ready, and I scream, "Where are you?"

My voice echoes throughout the house. She knows I've found my wife. She knows I'm ready.

And surely she must also know that she's about to die.

CHAPTER FORTY-TWO

I KEEP MY SHOTGUN RAISED, aimed at every corner. One hand steadies the weapon. The other keeps my finger over the trigger, ready to squeeze the instant I see movement. I'm ready for anything.

The open wound on Kacey's belly... The pain she would have been in...

Even though I know I've just searched each room, I do it again, nudging the spare room open with my knee first. The door creaks and I aim the shotgun from one corner to the next. Under the table, the other side of the bed, inside the cupboard.

Her face... Her mouth open... Her eyes still...

I leave the room, run down the stairs, and scan the hallway. Through to the kitchen, where I use my foot to open cupboards she could be hiding in, and use my back to open the door to the utility room. I am just about to enter the living room when I hear it.

Outside. On the driveway. A rustle, like someone stepping on leaves.

I run to the front door, open it slightly, and wait.

I want to mutilate this fucker, but I have to get her first. I can't be reckless. Must be smart. Must take it slowly.

She killed my wife... My wife... She cut her throat and waited for her to bleed out...

I grip the gun harder. My rage intensifies. I am trying so damn hard not to be reckless, but I just want to charge out there, find her, destroy her…

The blood on the sheets...

Stop thinking about her.

Stop it.

Please, stop it.

She will have suffered.

Fuck it.

I kick the door open and burst onto the driveway.

"Where are you!" I roar.

I turn my shotgun to the right. To the left.

It's dark, but the moonlight will illuminate any movement.

But there is none.

I pace toward the garage, open it, and look around.

"Where are you!"

I march back across the driveway, searching, really wanting to squeeze that trigger.

The gate that leads to the back garden is open.

A sting of satisfaction seizes through me, and I can't help but smile.

"I got you!"

I run. No cautious steps, no careful scanning – I run, hard, into the back garden, not wanting her to be able to climb over a fence or find a new hiding place, and I come to a sudden halt as soon as I enter, waiting to see where she is, waiting to aim my gun, and–

She's not there.

"Fuck's sake!"

I kick a potted plant. It hurts but it smashes the pot and I feel better for a moment.

Just for a moment.

I lift my gun and aim it at one corner of the garden, then the other, waiting for movement behind plants or a flicker of movement behind the bench.

Still nothing.

I walk further into the garden. There is a light coming from inside the house. In the living room.

It looks like a phone screen.

Adrenaline swarms through my veins like locusts. I shove the kitchen door open, run through, and enter the living room, and aim my gun, and–

She is not there. But my lost phone is. It's propped up against the television.

And there's a video playing on it.

I approach it.

It's me on the video. From ten, fifteen minutes ago. My car skids to a halt on the driveway, I kick the door open, and charge at the front door.

The video was taken from across the street. She was stood there the whole time, watching me, *filming* me…

On my own damn phone…

I struggle to contain myself. I struggle not to scream and punch the wall and trash the room. I want to kill this whore so much I can't contain my fury.

As it is, all I can do is watch the video, watching myself attempting to turn the front door handle as I find it locked, as I fumble for my keys, as my arms shake, as I struggle to open the door amid my anger.

"Kacey!" I hear myself shout.

She doesn't enter the house. Instead, she walks to the windows, and she films me from outside as I knock the shoe rack over and try to put the light on and stumble into the living room.

She is metres from me. That is all. Outside, in the shadows, filming as I move through the living room.

Then I run upstairs.

And you can no longer hear me, but I know what's happening off screen.

And the movie ends.

And I let out a scream that's so hard my throat gives way and cuts it off.

I aim my gun at the phone and I shoot and I miss and pieces of television fly in every direction, and the phone falls to the floor.

And I stand there.

Panting. Sweat dripping off me. My t-shirt is drenched.

I want to trash something else. I want to destroy the entire home that we built. Yet I can't move.

And that's when I hear it.

From behind me.

So subtle that, if it weren't for my momentary break in movement, I wouldn't be able to hear it.

A soft step on the carpet.

And I know she's there.

CHAPTER FORTY-THREE

I DON'T LIFT my gun. I don't make it obvious that I know. I keep it at waist height, but with both hands still on it, ready to fire in her direction as soon as I'm able.

I begin to rotate. Like I'm heading to the door. And I make a step toward it.

Something flies past my head. It hits the wall and lands on the floor. It looks like a dart. A sedative, maybe.

I turn around.

And I look upon the face of the slut who did this to me.

My lip curls. A rush flows through me. I have never been so furious and so happy at the same time.

She holds a rifle in one hand, and a dart in the other that she's not able to load quickly enough.

And she just stares at me.

Me, with the shotgun pointed at her.

And neither of us move.

She looks worse. Thin, but too thin. Her bones press against her skin. Bags under her eyes. Greasy hair.

Oh, my darling, you should have gone to the police.

She looks at the door to the living room, and through the

hallway, to where she can see the front door. I see her decision-making. I see her mind working it out.

Can she make it before I fire my gun?

Try it.

Go on, try it.

She doesn't.

Neither of us say anything, but in our eyes we say all we need to.

She is one mad bitch. It's in the way she looks at me, that desire for vengeance, that resolve. She's prepared to die right now, there's no doubt about that.

But I don't just want to kill her.

I want to *murder* her. To *mutilate* her. To *butcher* her.

And so I wait for her to make a move. And she waits for me. And we remain in this stand-off.

I lick my lips.

I'm going to make sure I enjoy this.

Her foot flinches. It points toward the door. She gives herself away. She's getting ready to make a run for it.

Is she faster than a shotgun shell?

I guess we'll find out.

Kacey's eyes. Empty. Throat sliced. Stab wound in her belly. Blood over the sheets. Long moments of suffering as she realised she was about to die.

You're going to pay for this, you really are.

Her body twists. Her legs tense.

And she moves, sprinting hard, trying to make the few metres to the door.

But she doesn't make it.

I squeeze the trigger and the gun kicks back and she falls to the floor with her legs flailing and a cry leaving her lips.

I don't move. I wait for her to get up. But she doesn't. She just squirms, rolling, writhing, her face scrunched up, blood oozing from her skin.

A piece of flesh of her left arm is missing. Its bloody, but I didn't hit her anywhere fatal. I just skimmed her arm.

That's okay. It means I can take longer.

I stand over her. Enjoy the dominance of her wriggling on the floor between my legs.

She doesn't look up. The pain must be too much. But she hasn't even begun to suffer yet.

I step on her arm. Press down with the heel of my boot. She cries out, and it's a long cry, one that turns into a scream then a shriek then a murmur, and I enjoy every moan she gives me.

I kick the rifle away from her, along with the darts.

I collect my phone. Watch the video back. Show it to her.

"Clever," I say, and she doesn't look at me, she just stares at the door.

I take my phone, exit the video of myself, and notice something else on the screen. A photo. I open it.

It's Jonno.

Hanging upside down. His chest split open. A pool of blood beneath his head.

"This real?" I ask her.

She still doesn't look at me.

"Oi, is this real?"

Still nothing.

Her silence doesn't annoy me. I see enough pain in her face that I'm satisfied she's suffering.

"I said, is this real?"

I squeeze the wound with my thumb and she screams and I get a little hard.

Still, she says nothing.

"Tell you what," I say. "Why don't we go find out?"

I stand, grab her by the hair, and lift her to her feet, then drag her through the hallway and to my car.

CHAPTER FORTY-FOUR

I DRIVE, and she sits in the passenger seat, occasionally glancing at the sawn-off shotgun on my lap, knowing that any movement she makes will result in a bullet in her chest.

She slumps down in her seat, like a petulant teenager, staring away from me. I snort away a laugh. I've seen her naked. I've been inside of her. I know what kind of fuck she is. That gives a man power over a woman that a she is reluctant to give up.

Which is why, sometimes, you just have to take it.

I put the radio on. The late-night DJ is playing songs to make us happy. Katrina and the Waves tell us about how they are walking on sunshine and Marvin Gaye joins with Tammi Terrell to tell us about how there ain't no mountain high enough. The words will probably lose all their meaning to a woman who's clutching an open wound on her arm caused by the scrape of a gunshot. I'm glad she's in pain, but honestly, I'm a little disappointed about my aim. I could have done better.

I swing around another corner so she falls against the door

and hits her arm and she moans. I chuckle again. Now the radio is telling us about how heaven is a place on earth.

"Belinda Carlisle," I say.

She doesn't look at me, but I can see her frown.

"The artist. That's her name. You're probably too young to remember her. What are you, a millennial?"

I know she'd have been born in the nineties. I'm just trying to get a rise out of her. She remains quiet and doesn't take the bait.

"She comes from Carlisle, and she's the only person in Carlisle to top the US charts."

She bites her lip. Pain contorts her frown.

"Was nominated for a Grammy, but Whitney Houston beat her. Though they both had something in common – drugs. Whitney loved her crack, Belinda loved her coke. The main difference – it killed Whitney, but Belinda, she carried on going for thirty years, snorting that shit up. You know what lesson we can learn from that?"

I turn and look at her. Grin at how she's trying to ignore me.

"Do coke instead of crack."

I burst out laughing. At first, it's to annoy her, then it becomes genuine, and I am in a fit of hysterics, completely taken by the hilarity of something that's just not that hilarious.

Then I remember what this woman did to Kacey, and I'm not laughing anymore.

I turn a corner and we pass a field of cows. I had to stop here a few weeks ago because one of them was in the middle of the road. I'd have just gone straight into it, but it would have wrecked my car. I made sure the farmer knew about how pissed off I was the next day.

"You probably think I'm evil, don't you?"

No reaction. Not an obvious one, anyway. But I can see her, churning over my words, trying to bide her time. She thinks the fight isn't over, and that she's going to have another chance to get me.

She's ridiculous.

And I am going to gauge out her eyeballs.

After all, Exodus preaches an eye for an eye.

"What I did to you was natural. What Jonno did to you was natural. But what you did to Kacey…"

I turn away. Run my hand down my face. Try to keep my cool.

"Well, that's fucked up. Killing and fucking is what animals do – but torture? For no other reason than for the pleasure of it? I mean, I gave your husband a quick death. You're lucky I was so kind."

She flinches.

She wants to spit back. I can see it. I almost have her. She'll open her mouth at any moment and I'll have broken her.

"Your husband was a squealer, weren't he? I mean, I've had my dick in a few arses in my time, but no one's ever squealed like he did."

I turn to look at her.

"You were nothing like your husband. You didn't squeal at all. You laid there and took it like a good little girl, didn't you?"

I put a hand on her leg.

"Daddy was proud of you."

She smacks my hand and I reach across her and grab her left arm and squeeze, hard, then harder still, her blood oozing between my fingers, trickling down my sleeve, thick and beautiful, and she screams, and finally I can hear her voice.

"You're a fucking tease. All you rich city fucks are teases. You're no better than nature; you just want to be fucked by a brute then fucked all over again."

She scrunches up her face and puts all her energy into not giving me the screams I desire.

"You're not better than any other rich bitch – don't you forget that."

We reach Jonno's estate and I let go.

She places a hand over her arm. The bleeding had stopped, but now it's gushing out again, dripping over my car seat. Once I've broken her, I'll make her clean it off with her tongue.

We reach Jonno's estate. We pass burnt-out cars and houses with St. George flags hanging out the window and empty beer cans on grass verges.

I pull up outside Jonno's house. I kill the engine. And I sit there.

"So where abouts is he?" I ask.

She's still grabbing her arm. Squirming. Scrunching up her face.

"Just scream, it'll feel better."

She glares at me.

"Fine, don't. Where is he?"

She doesn't answer.

I reach across to grab her arm again, and she quickly turns away and answers, "The garage."

My gaze lifts to the garage straight ahead of us.

"And how'd you do it?" I ask.

She doesn't answer.

"You used his loneliness, didn't you?"

She doesn't answer.

"You made him think you loved him. Then you killed him. Didn't you?"

She stares at me, but still doesn't answer. In her eyes, I see the same kind of rage I have to contain every damn day. I strike her head with the butt of my shotgun, and blood trickles down her nose. I strike her again, and again, until she's unconscious, and I am sure she's not going anywhere.

I step out of the car, and approach the garage.

CHAPTER FORTY-FIVE

I GIVE the garage door a nudge. It's unlocked. I nudge it harder until it's open.

I can see the silhouette in the darkness. Upside down.

And it stinks. Like rotting flesh and rotting shit and rotten eggs and rotting cabbage – just a mixture of rot. And a slight tinge of garlic.

It's the kind of smell that gets stuck in your nostrils; that stays there and won't ever go away.

I flick the light.

I almost gag.

I almost gag.

I gag at nothing, but at this, I want to retch.

I glance over my shoulder. She's in the car. Watching me. Is she enjoying this?

I turn back to the body. It's been here for days. His chest is open and pieces of his insides – I have no idea what parts of him they are – rest half out of his body. The blood that remains on his body has crusted. The blood on the floor has stained the surface. His face is barely recognisable.

I turn away. Pinch my nostrils. Tell myself it's nothing, and I'm hard as fuck, and I can look at a stupid dead body.

But this isn't just a dead body. It's a corpse. A carcass. Mangled, mutilated remains of some sick and twisted woman's whim.

I look back at the car. I can only see the outline of her body in the darkness. I want to shout at her, *You did this? You? What the fuck is wrong with you?*

What we did to her was *nothing* compared to this.

She bound Kacey to the bed and slit her throat and hung Jonno upside down and cut his body open and left them both to die, and what was she planning for me?

I'm the worst. I'm the ringleader. If she was willing to do this to them, then what was she willing to do to me?

I glare at the darkness where her outline rests.

I want to ask her how she thought she was going to get one over on Pitbull.

Pitbull, who's hard as fucking nails.

Pitbull, who doesn't take shit from anyone.

Pitbull, who *no one* fucks with.

I charge back to the car. Swing the car door open.

"What were you going to do to me, huh? What were you going to do?"

I grab her neck. Her head slumps to the side. I want her to be awake to witness what I'm going to do to her. I want her conscious and alert as she suffers the pain of a slow, cruel death. I am not having her unconscious!

I stride to Jonno's front door, go to barge it open, then try the door, and find that she left it unlocked. I stride to the kitchen, where Jonno's dirty plates are stacked high in the sink.

I grab a washing up bowl that he hardly ever used and fill it with cold water. I find ice cubes in the freezer and put all of them in the bowl. If I am going to wake her up with this, I am going to need the water to be freezing.

I pick up the bowl, trying to keep it steady, and pause.

There's a picture on the wall of Jonno and me. Years ago, in Magaluf. Bright sunshine firing down upon us as we stand in our trunks, in the middle of the sea. Kacey is there in her bikini, her body looking stunning like it always does.

I ignored his calls. I blamed all of this on him.

Whilst I should have been blaming it on *her*.

"Sorry, mate," I grumble as I take one last look at the picture and return to the driveway.

The bowl is hard to balance when I walk too fast, so I slow down, approaching the car cautiously, trying to avoid spilling any. Each step is too long, but it's necessary.

The smell hits me again and I glance over my shoulder at Jonno and it just makes me all the more motivated to destroy her.

I am going to chop her fingers off and fuck her with them.

I am going to slice off her hair until she's bald as a baby.

I am going to mangle her cunt and shove a corkscrew inside of her and chop off her breasts and force her to eat my shit before finally ripping her throat apart with my bare hands.

My arms are shaking. I try to steady them. I've worked myself up too much.

I hold the bowl in one hand. Open the car door with the other, ready to wake her up.

Then I drop the bowl and the water goes everywhere.

"What the fuck…"

She isn't there.

I look at the backseat. The driver's seat.

She's gone.

And the glove compartment…

It's open.

And the grenades are missing.

And, just as the thought registers, I hear the tinkle of metal approach my feet.

CHAPTER FORTY-SIX

I RUN.

I know what one of my grenades sounds like.

I don't know how long I'm, running for – a seconds, maybe – but I get far enough away from the blast that it doesn't kill me, though I'm still taken from my feet and onto on my back.

I can't feel my legs.

I look down. There's a large chunk of my foot missing. Oh, God, it hurts.

I try to sit up but it's agony.

I can move my legs but every movement feels tender, like there's something I'm pulling every time I shift position.

I manage to lean up, but I can't get to my feet. Every movement of my arm sends a fiery pain through my muscles. I can barely move.

From the smoke, she emerges. The moon lights her face. It's blank and brutal. Without expression, yet full of rage. It's the expression I've worn my entire life.

"Please…" I whimper, and I'd made no conscious decision to do so, and I feel like a fool, and I tell myself not to beg for my life.

I beg to no one.

But fear takes over. A will to live. A desperation to survive. And begging is all I can do.

"Please, please don't, please, I–"

She reaches my side. Looks me in the eye, then stamps on my wounded foot.

I scream, and I can't stop screaming. It's too much. The pain is too much. I can't take it.

"Please, I'm sorry, I–"

She stamps on it again and I scream and she's enjoying this, isn't she?

The sick bitch.

She's actually enjoying this.

"What is wrong with you?" I ask.

She stamps on my leg again and I holler and moan and I turn, onto my front, and I try dragging myself across the road, but my arms are too tender, and I can't even shift an inch.

People look out of their windows. They can see me begging. They can see me pleading for my life.

Are they phoning the police?

Jesus. Now I'm wanting the filth to help me. What has she done to me...

But they don't call the police around here.

Even if a grenade goes off, it's not that kind of estate.

It's the kind of estate where you sort your problems out yourself.

It's the kind of estate where you mind your own business.

It's the kind of estate where a psychotic whore can get away with bloody fucking murder.

I try to drag myself away, but in truth, I can't endure the pain it takes to move.

I look behind me.

She's watching me. Just standing there, enjoying my pain. She relishes the sight.

"Leave me alone!" I say and I turn and I crawl away, determined to withstand the pain, inching forward, but I have to stop as I'm struggling to breathe. I'm panting and wheezing and each breath is becoming an effort too much for me.

"Please…"

I'm not even sure what I'm begging for anymore.

For her to let me go, or for her to put me out of my misery?

She saunters toward me. There's a sexiness to her stride that I resent. I've never been turned on by an empowered woman. I like them subservient.

But this is as empowered as a woman can ever be.

"I'm sorry…"

She snorts a laugh. Like the way I snorted a laugh when I was driving earlier. I don't know if it's genuine or if she's mimicking me.

"What I did was wrong, I know that now…"

She puts her feet beside my armpits and stands over my body.

"I shouldn't have done it…"

She mounts me in a way that would have turned me on a day ago, but now makes me quiver as I stare the potential of death in the face.

"You're not a monster… Please…"

But she is a monster.

Have you seen what she's already done?

There's no other word to describe her other than *monster*.

I go to speak but she tells me to shut up.

I obey.

She grabs my head. Lifts it back. Then slams it against the cement.

It all goes fuzzy.

She lifts my head back again, then slams it another time.

It knocks me out, and now I am truly at her mercy.

CHAPTER FORTY-SEVEN

THE WORLD RETURNS IN FLASHES.

A scrape of the floor. A drag from here to there. A shove into wherever.

I have no idea where I am or where I'm going.

Kacey taunts me. I see her in my mind as if she's right before me, asking me why I'm so pathetic. It's a good question.

How did I let her beat me?

I'm Pitbull. I don't let people beat me.

But you let HER beat you.

I'm sorry.

She killed me, and now she'll kill you.

It isn't my fault.

Jacob, my darling – this is ALL your fault.

I begin to stir. I don't know how long it's been, but there's light. My eyes flicker open. The sun is at the high point of the sky. There's green and there's hills.

I don't know where I am.

I close my eyes again. Feel my body fall limp.

A bucket of freezing cold water makes them open again, and I am suddenly alert, looking one way then the other.

And I am in a completely different place, with no idea how much time has passed.

I am stood in front of a tree with a noose around my neck. I look up. It's tied to a sturdy branch.

I look around and she's there and I try to charge at her, but I fall over.

There's rope around my ankles. They are bound together. My hands are cuffed behind my back. The other end of the noose is attached to this tree.

I am going nowhere.

I try screaming, but I know it's useless. I'm in a field, and I can see into all the other fields, and the fields beyond that. There is no one nearby.

I have lost.

She sits on the bonnet of my car, watching me. Fascinated by my behaviour. Like a scientist studying a lab rat.

"Please…" My voice sounds like a child. "Please just let me go…"

She laughs. I don't blame her.

"Please… I'll do anything…"

She raises her eyebrows and finishes her banana. "Anything?"

I nod my head eagerly.

"Yes, anything."

She sticks out her bottom lip as if contemplating this. I can't tell if she's genuinely considering letting me go or mocking me.

"You've made your point. What I did was bad. Awful. It really was. You showed that to Jonno and Kacey, and now you've shown it to me. Is that what you want? You've won. I'm scum."

"Worse than scum."

"Fine, I'm worse than scum. I am the shit on the bottom of a shoe.

"Worse."

"I am the shit of the fly that eats the shit.

"Still worse."

"I am the rats that carry the plague. I am the bogie a toddler flicks, the stink of a fat man's fart, the fucking arsehole of Hitler's fucking arse. I know that now! I do!"

She leaps off the bonnet. Takes my shotgun. Aims it at me.

"You don't even know how to fire that," I say.

"You want me to try?"

I shake my head. "No. No, I don't."

She licks her lips. Watches me.

"If you want to survive, you will do everything I tell you. Do you understand?"

"Then will you let me go?"

"Of course."

She smiles. I don't like that smile.

"How do I know you're telling the truth?"

"You're not in the position to doubt me."

She has a point.

"Okay. Right. Fair enough, okay, I'll do what you say."

"Perfect. Now pull your trousers down."

"What? I thought you were going to let me go?"

"After you pull your trousers down…"

I try to move my hands. It's tough to do anything while they are bound behind my back.

"I can't," I tell her.

"If you really want me to let you go, you'll find a way."

I feel for my belt, grip it, and give my trousers a little push, and I nudge them halfway down my arse.

I wriggle and writhe, hopping up and down, moving back and forth, doing whatever I can to force my trousers to slide slowly down my legs, wincing as I make contact with my foot.

She's laughing. Whatever. She can laugh. I don't care. I want to live.

I really want to live.

They reach my thighs and I hop, moving them slightly with each shuffle. I jump with more vigour and they reach my knees, and I jump some more and they drop to my ankles.

"There! I did it. Now will you–"

"And the boxers."

"What?"

She raises her eyebrows. She does not want to repeat herself.

"Fine. You want to humiliate me. I humiliated you, so it's payback. I get it. Then will you let me go?"

She doesn't answer.

"Will you let me go?"

She still doesn't answer.

"Fine. I'll do it. Whatever."

I arch my back and push the waist band of my underwear down. I wriggle to the right then the left and to the right and the left again, and they fall, and my big, floppy cock waves around.

I've never realised how stupid this makes a man look. I've seen Kacey wearing just a t-shirt and nothing else before. She looks sexy. Me, wearing a t-shirt and nothing on my bottom half, I look pitiful.

"I'm done," I tell her. "Can you let me go now?"

My cheeks are wet. I'm crying. I can hear Kacey telling me to grow up. I don't care anymore.

"Please…"

She opens the car door and puts the shotgun inside.

I breathe a sigh of relief.

Then she takes out the second grenade.

"What – what are you doing with that?"

She skips over to me like a child in a playground.

"What are you doing?"

She stands beside me. Looks down my legs, over my naked rear-end, and smiles a smile that scares me.

"What are you doing?"

"Bend over," she tells me.

"I thought you were letting me go."

She smiles. Waves me closer and leans forward until her lips meet my ear. With the warmth of her breath against my skin, she whispers, "I lied."

She bends me over and before I know it the tip of the grenade is halfway into my arsehole.

"Stop!"

She shoves it harder in and it scrapes and it's too big to fit into such a tiny hole but she shoves it in anyway, harder and harder.

"Please stop!"

Halfway in and it feels like a melon being through me.

"Please stop, I can't take it, I–"

I can't speak anymore because I'm screaming. I'm not sure but I might hear her laughing and it's going in harder and she's shoving it, batting her hand against the end like she's trying to shove a cricket stump into the ground.

I try to plead again but it turns to wails as the entire grenade penetrates the tender walls of my rectum.

All of it except the pin, which pokes out.

"Please, please don't remove that pin, please don't, I–"

She removes the pin.

"Fuck! You whore! You fucking slut! You fucking whore slut stupid fucking cunt! You deserved everything you got you fucking snobby cunt you fucking cunt I hate you you fucking cunt!"

She smirks. "That all?"

She saunters back to the car, her hips swaying back and forth.

I try to stand, and I manage to rise up with crooked knees.

I use the rope around my neck to keep myself balanced, and it is the only thing holding me up.

She opens the car door and removes the shotgun, then backs up until she is far enough not to get hurt by the grenade.

Then she aims it at the rope that holds me to the tree.

"No!" I beg. "Please no! Please, please no!"

She holds the gun well. Makes sure her aim is perfect. Readies her finger on the trigger.

I am bawling my eyes out. This could be the last few seconds of my life unless I convince her not to.

"Please, I'm sorry…"

"Sorry? I thought I was a snobby cunt?"

"I didn't mean it, I…"

It's no good. It's over. I'm done.

"Fine! You are a snobby cunt! And I'm glad I fucked your husband and broke his neck!"

She squeezes the trigger. It shoots through the rope and my body falls and I hop, trying to keep myself on my feet, and I think I have myself balanced but it's too uncomfortable and I fall onto my side and I look her in the eyes and–

And then the grenade explodes, and pieces of my body scatter themselves all over the hills of Frome.

PART IV
THE BEGINNING

CHAPTER FORTY-EIGHT

THE GRAVE IS STILL the same. It doesn't change.

It doesn't grow grey hair or require a hearing aid or spend time with its grandchildren or write Christmas cards or pay off the mortgage.

It's just a stone. A piece of rock with letters on it. The letters don't matter; they have the same cliché as any other piece of useless rock.

But it's where his ashes are buried.

And that's why it matters.

She runs her hands down the lettering, feeling the bumps in the surface and pretending they are the contours of his face. The first letter is the dip of his eyes and the next letter is the crook of his nose and the raindrop hanging off the final word is the moisture of his lips.

She doesn't know what to say. Sorry? I love you? Goodbye?

Does any of it mean anything anyway?

It's raining.

It's been raining for a while, but she's only just realised.

There's an elderly couple visiting the grave of their son a

few stones over. She sees them here a lot. They come as often as she does, but she never says hello.

Hello will lead to a conversation. A conversation will lead to sharing. Sharing will lead to caring.

And she's not sure she has it in her to care anymore.

Somewhere out there, there are three more graves, for three people who committed the worst crimes imaginable.

Or maybe there aren't any graves. If no one cares enough to buy a grave, do they get one? If no one cares enough to keep their ashes, are they just brushed into a dustbin and taken out with the rest of the trash?

There's a woman sat on a bench. A woman who sits there every day. Who brings sandwiches. Who offered her one once. She didn't reply.

Where does she go from here, after all?

Does she just have sandwiches on a bench like she can do normal things?

Does she go to work and spend time with colleagues and have trauma counselling? Does she date again? Remarry?

What would be the alternative?

Killing more people? Those that deserve it, maybe. A crusade of vengeance for women who've been wronged, only stopping when she's caught or killed. She could become a figure of justice for all the women out there who saw their husband…

Saw their husband what?

She still can't say it. Can she?

Not even think it.

And what of what she did? Can she think or speak of that?

No. But it's all she ever sees. In her nightmares. In her thoughts. Lying there at the back of her mind like a stalker outside your window.

The truth is, it's never over.

You never recover.

Some go on to lead fulfilling lives.

Some keep the damage hidden and pretend to be able to have the same healthy relationships that other people are capable of.

And some cry and moan and have sex with strangers because all they think they can offer someone is their body.

Truth is, she can't even offer anyone that anymore. Her skin has faded and her bones are prominent and her muscles are small. Her body is just as mistreated as her mind.

She stands. Kisses her hand and rests it on the stone.

The elderly couple across from her smile, as if they understand.

She frowns because they don't, and they avert their gaze.

And she leaves.

Who knows where to, or how she'll get there, or why she'll go there.

She will carry her actions with her wherever she goes.

Maybe she'll give up. Maybe not tomorrow, but maybe the next day.

Or maybe she won't.

Because, despite all of what has occurred, she still wants to live. She wants a life. What's left of it, that is.

She just doesn't know what she wants to do with that life.

She walks down the narrow path and passes the bushes and crosses the car park.

His mother called her yesterday. Wants to make sure she's all right. Wants to stay in touch because her son was fond of her.

But that person her son loved… She's lost.

She's still back there in that cottage screaming as they torture her husband.

This woman is someone else.

Something else.

She pauses as she hears the aggressive voice of a nearby man. Searches for its source.

Outside a pub, a man shouts at a woman. She watches them as the woman tells him to leave her alone and he says that he's sick of her acting like this. He punches the wall because he thinks punching the wall instead of her makes him a better man.

She watches him.

Then she reaches into her pocket and feels for the knife.

And she's grateful to him.

Because he's just showed her who she's going to be.

He's just given her reason to keep living.

And she knows just how to repay him.

JOIN RICK WOOD'S READER'S GROUP...

And get **Roses Are Red So Is Your Blood** for free!

Join at **www.rickwoodwriter.com/sign-up**

AVAILABLE IN THE BLOOD SPLATTER
BOOKS SERIES...

Psycho B*tches
Shutter House
This Book is Full of Bodies
Haunted House
Home Invasion
Woman Scorned

BLOOD SPLATTER BOOKS

18+

SHUTTER HOUSE

RICK WOOD

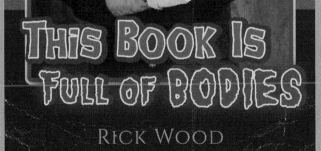

BLOOD SPLATTER BOOKS

18+

This Book Is Full of BODIES

RICK WOOD

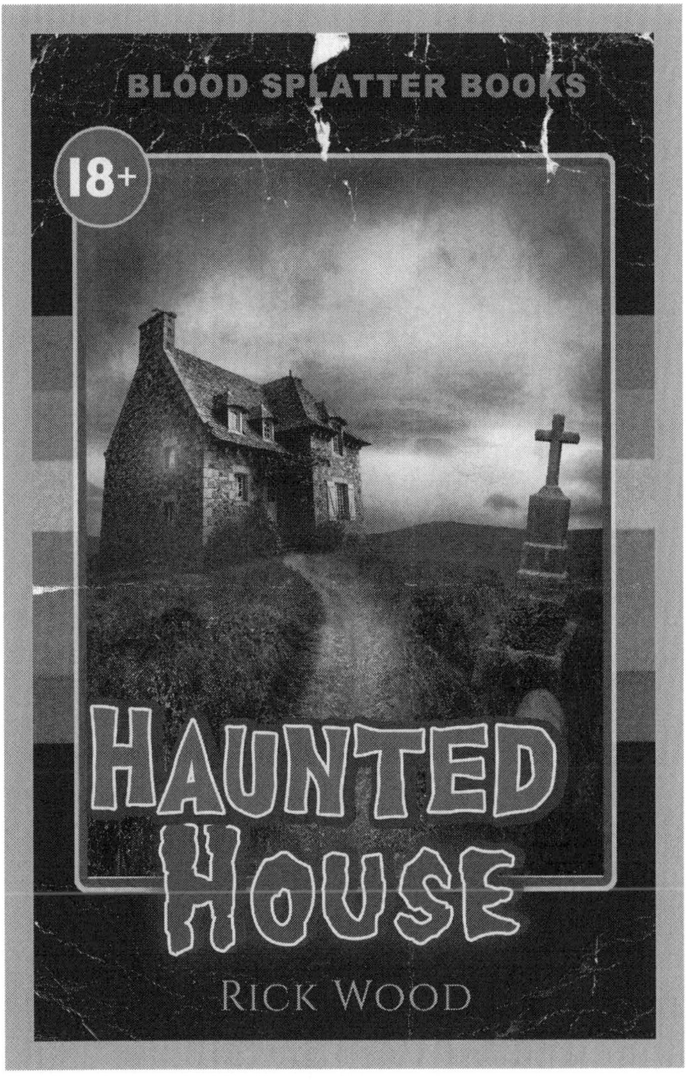
BLOOD SPLATTER BOOKS
18+
HAUNTED HOUSE
RICK WOOD

BLOOD SPLATTER BOOKS

18+

HOME
INVASION

RICK WOOD

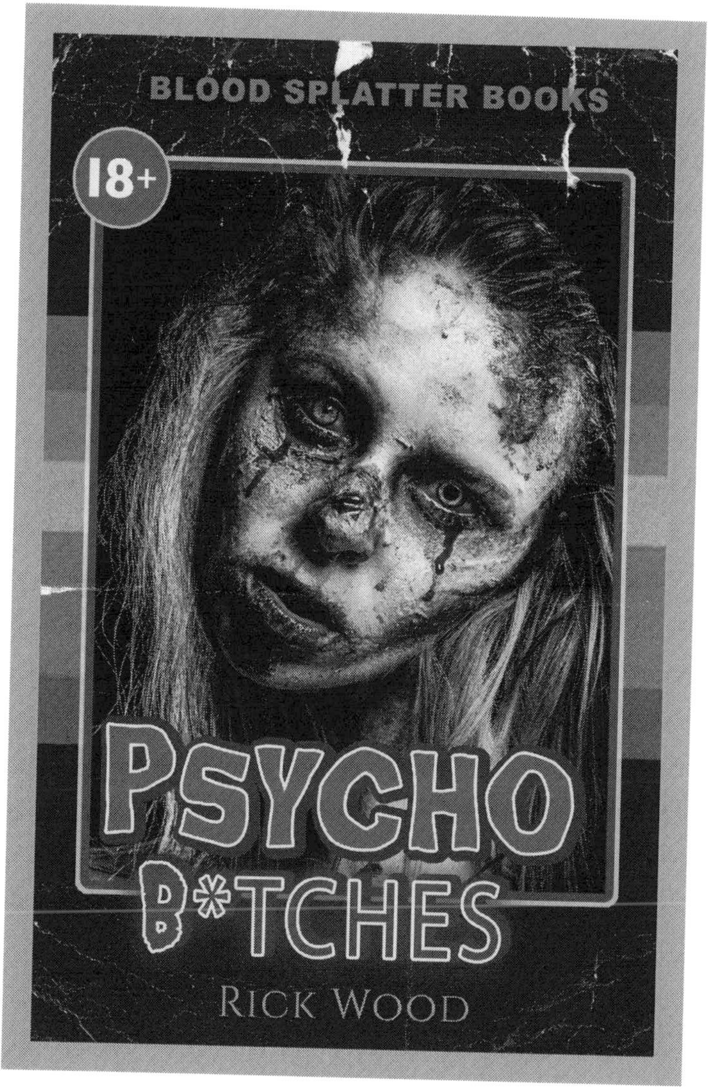
BLOOD SPLATTER BOOKS
18+
PSYCHO
B*TCHES
RICK WOOD

ALSO BY RICK WOOD...

BOOK ONE IN THE SENSITIVES SERIES

THE SENSITIVES

RICK WOOD

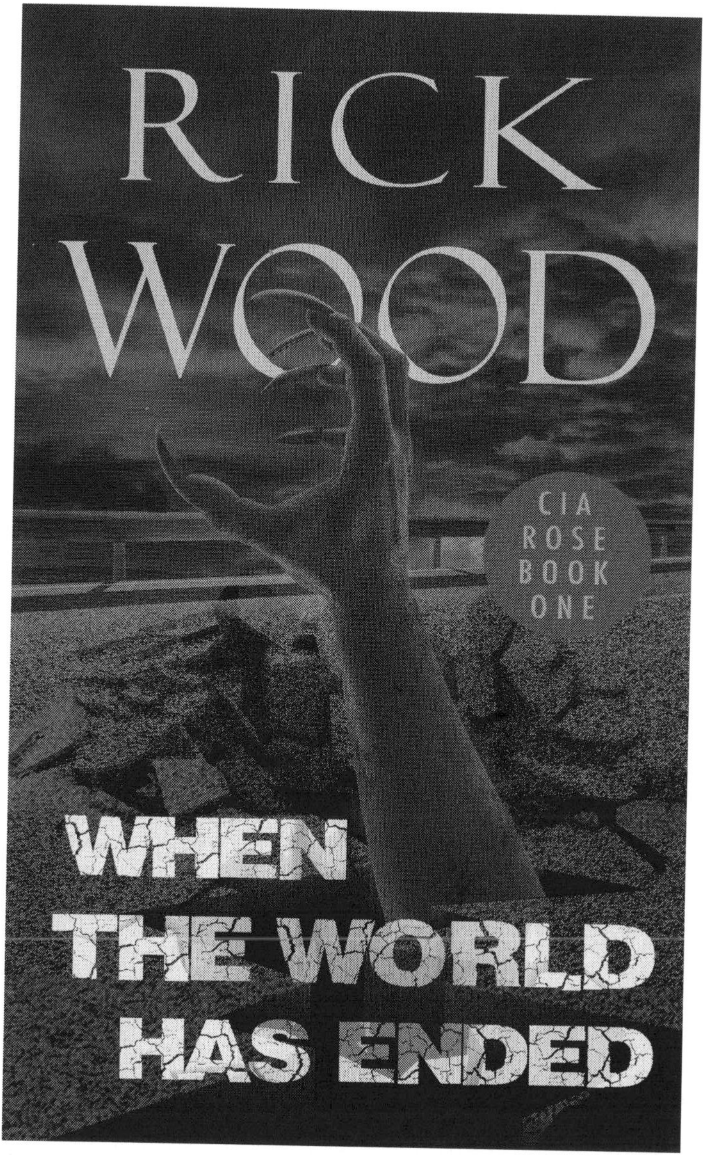
RICK
WOOD
CIA
ROSE
BOOK
ONE
WHEN
THE WORLD
HAS ENDED

Made in the USA
Las Vegas, NV
30 October 2021